THE MONSTER IN THE LAKE

LOUIE STOWELL

nosy crow

First published in the UK in 2020 by Nosy Crow Ltd
The Crow's Nest, 14 Baden Place
Crosby Row, London, SE1 1YW, UK

www.nosycrow.com

ISBN: 978 1 78800 045 1

Nosy Crow and associated logos are trademarks and/or registered
trademarks of Nosy Crow Ltd

A CIP catalogue record for this book is available from the
British Library.

Printed and bound in Great Britain by Clays Ltd, Elcograf S.p.A.

Papers used by Nosy Crow are made from wood grown in sustainable forests

3 5 7 9 10 8 6 4 2

To my parents.
L.S.

To my friend Stella.
D.O.

THIS NEW NOTEBOOK BELONGS TO JOSH. HANDS OFF IF YOU ARE NOT JOSH. IF YOU *ARE* JOSH, PLEASE READ ON.

IF YOU ARE ALITA OR KIT YOU CAN READ OVER MY SHOULDER IF YOU LIKE BUT NO ADDING ANYTHING.

AND IF YOU ARE KIT, NO GETTING DIRT ON THIS BOOK. IT IS NEW!

Dear Future Josh,

You will probably have many exciting things happen to you in the future, where you live, so here are a few notes so you don't forget the exciting things that have already happened.

By the way, are you prime minister yet? Did you stop global warming? Are you a famous writer? I can't wait to get to the future to find out!

So here's what's happened recently. At the start of the summer holidays, our friend Kit discovered that she's a wizard - the youngest one in the world as far as I know, and I know a lot. Me and Alita discovered that we aren't wizards (boo), but we did help to save the world (yay). Here are some other important facts you need to know about wizards, and about our summer so far...

1) Wizards are real but they don't all have long white beards or pointy hats. They DO have cloaks though, and our local wizard, Faith Braithwaite, wears a lot of dangly star earrings and very

bright lipstick.

2) Every wizard has a second job: running a library. This is because underneath every library sleeps a dragon. If that dragon wakes up, terrible things happen. So when a librarian tells you to "shh" in a library, it's to save the world from fire and chaos, not because they're trying to spoil your fun.

3) At the start of the summer holidays, an evil businessman called Hadrian Salt tried to wake the dragon under our library because he wanted to use its power to become a wizard. Me, Kit, Alita and Faith stopped him using magic, books and our brains. My brain in particular.

4) Some books in our library are

magical, and I'm not allowed to read them out loud unless Faith is there - book spells are so powerful that the spells can start working even if you're not a wizard. There are other magical books too, called portal books. You can use them to travel huge distances between libraries.

Portal books are also really fun because it's like you're inside the book. For example, there's one that's a book about gardening and you get to walk through all these beautiful gardens. The ones with dangerous animals and monsters in aren't as fun though, because you have to run, and I don't like running. My brain is mightier than my legs.

5) Beneath the library is a forest

called the Book Wood. It's also known as the Stacks, and it's where all the really magical books are kept. Over time, some of those books turned back into trees, and their pages turned into trunks and leaves, covered in spells. I am DEFINITELY not allowed to read the spells on the book trees. They're some of the most powerful spells in existence, and apparently I might blow myself up. Kit's not allowed to read them either because she's only a trainee wizard. But that's not much of a risk because she's more likely to want to climb a tree than read one.

6) I think that's it. Oh wait, no. I haven't said anything about the dragon who sleeps beneath our library. She's called Draca, and it's part of our job to read to her – it helps her stay asleep

and makes sure her dreams are full of stories. You can climb into Draca's dream with her to talk to her. She doesn't always make sense but she's a friendly dragon, not a scary one.

7) Me and Alita have been helping Kit to train to become a wizard – along with Faith, who's doing most of the teaching, because Kit is too young to go to the Wizard Academy. Kit's getting better at magic but she still makes a lot of mistakes. She also doesn't like reading so it's up to me and Alita to learn all about how magic works so we can tell her when she's wrong.

Josh out!

PS: Josh forgot to add that there's a half-dragon, half-dog who lives *in the library, called Dogon. Dogon is the sweetest little creature that ever lived. He breathes the cutest fire. Also, it's mostly Josh who's always telling Kit she's wrong.*

Alita xxx

I TOLD YOU NO ADDING ANYTHING, ALITA! AND I DON'T ALWAYS TELL KIT SHE'S WRONG, ONLY WHEN SHE IS WRONG!

PPS come on guys, you've been riting in that notebook for practically HOURS, let's go and do something fun. This is the summer holidays not skool!

kit

KIT, THIS IS MY BOOK. STOP

WRITING IN IT! YOU DON'T EVEN
LIKE WRITING! YOU DIDN'T EVEN
SPELL 'WRITING' RIGHT! AND WE
CAN GO OUTSIDE WHEN I AM
DONE.

OK. I AM DONE.

*Josh out again, with this notebook
going in a SAFE place this time.*

CHAPTER 1

MISS-
SPELLINGS

In the Book Wood beneath the library, Kit Spencer was practising spells. She was a stocky girl, with red hair, pale skin and more mud than you'd usually see on a person who wasn't a professional pig wrestler.

At that moment, Kit was wearing her (not-yet-muddy) wizard's cloak and hovering a ball of fire above her head. Her tongue was out, and her face was screwed up in concentration. The goal was to raise the fireball above her head, then lower it to the ground. So far, so good...

Faith was guiding her through the spell. The librarian was a tall, dark-skinned black woman, with ever-so-slightly-sarcastic eyebrows. She was wearing a long, fluorescent-yellow dress and a chunky blue necklace. Her hair was in long locs, and her elegant nails were painted the same electric blue as her necklace. Unlike Kit, she wasn't wearing a cloak: mostly wizards only wore those for ceremonies and parties. But as a wizard in training, Kit wore hers to track her progress. Each time she learned a new spell, her cloak gained an extra stripe of yellow at the bottom. She currently had a band of yellow about the width of her hand.

She was hoping that, any moment, she'd be getting her Controlled Fireball spell stripe. She was so close!

Faith was standing beside Kit, watching the fireball intently. "Now, slowly … use the gesture I showed you … and slowly, slowly lift the ball a few inches. That's it. Gently…"

Kit was concentrating so hard that her forehead was a wall of sweat. This was the hardest spell she'd tried so far. The words of the spell weren't hard: just a quick "*Feuer, oben*" at the beginning. But after that, you had to focus your mind so hard it felt like you were going to burst a blood vessel somewhere deep in your skull.

Now, in this moment, Kit could feel the magic flowing through her as she focused on the fire, keeping it in its ball shape, keeping it steady...

She lifted her hands just a little. The fireball wobbled and dipped.

But then it rose, slowly, slowly...

Kit felt something new building inside her. She'd never managed to get this spell to work properly. Was this what it was supposed to feel like? It was intense! Almost painful...

"I'm doing it!" Kit cried. "I can feel it worki—"

At which point the fireball flew up into the air and exploded like a firework over the treetops, scattering light of every colour.

"AAAAAARGH!" Kit shrieked, shaking her hands as if they were on fire, then tripping on a root and tumbling backwards on to her bottom with a bone-jarring BUMP.

"Are you OK?"
Faith rushed forward
to help her up,

checking her over for injuries. "You're not burned, are you? Or in any way broken?"

"No, I … don't think so." Kit's bottom was bruised, but the heat of the spell had all flown upwards. She peered up above the trees to where the fireball had exploded.

"Where did it go?" she asked.

Faith waved a hand above them. "There are protection spells above the trees, to stop any rogue magic damaging the library above. They absorbed your fireball spell." She smiled. "So don't worry, it's safe to make mistakes down here."

Kit screwed up her brow. "The thing is, I thought the spell was working. I mean … it *was* working. I just don't know what went wrong. Something felt … weird." She looked down at her cloak. No new yellow stripe. Her heart sank.

"Well," said Faith, "it's a bright sunny day out there – maybe you got distracted? I'm guessing you actually want to be outside? Maybe you need a break?"

Kit felt annoyed. Sure, yes, she *did* have a habit of getting distracted. And yes, it was a sunny

August afternoon and every other child her age was outside in the park or at the swimming pool. But she *hadn't* got distracted. Not this time.

Faith picked up the pile of books they'd been using and ushered her towards the exit of the Book Wood. "Come on. I think that's enough work for today. Break time."

"I *didn't* just get distracted, though," said Kit, not wanting Faith to think she was lazy. "I felt something. Just before it went wrong, I had this … this rush, here." She put her hand to her chest.

Faith gave her a curious look. "That doesn't sound right," she said. With the books balanced on the crook of one arm, she pulled something out of her pocket. It looked like a tiny silver flute but had a little blue gemstone at one end, instead of a mouthpiece. She pressed some little keys and the gemstone glowed red.

"What's that?" asked Kit.

"Thaumometer," said Faith. She held it away from her and waved it around, back and forth, in front of Kit. "It measures magic. Hmmm… The wild magic readings in the air are a bit high, even for down here near the dragon." She shook the thaumometer, and looked at it again. Its gemstones were lit up like a Christmas tree, and it emitted a faint hum. "Hmm… Perhaps it picked up the extra magic in my pocket. Too many magical objects in there; I must have a clear-out." She patted a large pocket in her dress, which lay flat against her hip and didn't appear to have anything in. But it rattled as she slapped it. Faith's pockets were like that. Infinitely full of stuff, but always looking empty. Kit had begged to learn the spell that made them like that, but Faith had told her it wasn't a specific spell – just what happens if you stuff enough magical items into a normal pocket, over time.

"Now, you go out into the sun and have fun. I have a meeting at the Wizards' Council to attend." She pulled some sunglasses out of the flat pocket. "Mustn't forget these."

The Wizards' Council were in charge of magic in England, Wales and Scotland, and all librarians had to attend meetings with them at least once a year. They were very old, very grumpy, and their meetings were so long and dull that Faith admitted she sometimes took a nap halfway through.

"The trick is wearing sunglasses," Faith had said. "They don't know you're asleep if they can't see your eyes."

Kit escaped into the sunshine, glad that she was only a trainee wizard for once.

CHAPTER 2

THE PARK

Once out in the warm, free air, Kit went to find her friends Alita and Josh. As she expected, they were lying underneath a tree, reading. Alita was curled up round her pile of books like a neatly-dressed dragon guarding a papery hoard. Her black hair was, as always, perfectly plaited, and her skin had the healthy brown glow of someone who always ate their fruit and vegetables without having to be bribed. In fact, she had a little container full of mango that her mum had packed her. Kit wasn't sure how it was physically possible, but Alita was managing to eat the mango while she read without getting yellowy-orange stains all over her pale blue dress.

Tall, skinny Josh had tight dark curls, brown skin, and an expression of extreme concentration. He was taking notes as he read. Josh never went anywhere without a notebook. He had an amazing memory, but insisted he needed to write everything down "for posterity". Kit wasn't sure, but she thought posterity had something to do with your bottom.

Josh was reading a book on Arthurian legends and wizard history, which Faith had found him from the Stacks. He'd put a blanket on the ground to lie on, partly to keep himself from getting grass stains, but also to protect the book.

Alita had her own rug and had spread out several books. She had the latest Danny Fandango – *Danny Fandango and the Crown of Bones*, which she'd just read for the fourth time that summer – and now she'd moved on to another, even fatter book, *The Lord of the Rings*. Kit thought a book that long would give you a permanent wrist injury. Trying to read it over Alita's shoulder certainly made Kit's brain feel injured.

"Hi, Kit!" said Josh. "Did you know King Arthur was actually a wizard, and Merlin wasn't?"

Kit told him she did not know that. She wasn't a hundred per cent sure she needed to, either.

"So," Josh went on, full of excitement about his new discoveries. "Merlin was a fake, who tried to steal Arthur's power! And Guinevere was a wizard too, only her story got covered up by history because back then people thought only men should be wizards."

"History sounds annoying," said Kit. "What are you reading, Alita?"

"I'm just up to the bit where Frodo arrives in Rivendell with the other hobbits and Strider," said Alita, as if Kit should know who any of those people or places were, or what a hobbit was.

"What's wrong?" asked Alita, seeing Kit's gloomy expression.

"My spell blew up," said Kit. "Big fireball, boom." She threw herself on the ground next to them, gaining some new grass stains on her knees, shorts and T-shirt in the process. "And now Faith probably thinks I'm lazy."

"What went wrong with the spell?" asked Alita.

"Did you get the hand gestures right?" asked Josh. He demonstrated the correct way of performing the gesture to lift the fireball.

"Yes!" said Kit. "I swear, I did."

"Even the bit where you lock your elbow?" asked Josh.

Alita nudged him. "Kit knows what she's doing, Captain Cleverclogs," she said.

"I do! I did it all right!" said Kit, with a grateful look at Alita. "But it was like the magic was misbehaving."

"Are you sure you didn't pronounce the words wrong?" asked Josh, giving her a sceptical look.

Kit rolled her eyes. "Fine, don't believe me. Let's go for a walk." She picked up Alita and Josh's books. "Wow, these are heavy."

"Not if you're sitting down reading them," said

Josh hopefully, not getting up.

But Kit stared until Josh and Alita reluctantly left their reading spot and picked up their blankets, and strolled down towards the lake to look at the ducks.

A dog walker was coming towards them. Kit

thought it looked like the best job in the world, just walking around the park with a pack of dogs. There was a German shepherd, a sausage dog carrying a stick in its mouth, a tiny Chihuahua, a big pit bull with the sweetest face that Kit had ever seen, and, all in all, more dogs than Kit could keep count of.

Alita was grinning even more widely than Kit.

"So. Many. Dogs," she whispered.

A large dog broke away and squatted down for a wee, and the pack came to a halt. The dog walker gave the children a toothy smile. "Would you like to say hello?" He gestured to the dogs. "They're all very friendly."

Alita didn't need asking twice. Cute dogs needed stroking. She got down on her knees, carefully laying down her enormous book on her folded blanket, and started stroking a fat little spaniel, scruffling its ears. Kit crouched down and started stroking the sausage dog. It was very wriggly and a little cross-looking. Being a walking sausage was apparently a very difficult life.

Josh was less delighted than the girls. "What if they lick me?" he said distrustfully.

"That's exactly the point!" said Alita. "Awww, this one's licking my face!"

"That's not hygienic," muttered Josh.

As the two girls were on their knees, stroking

several dogs each, and giggling as the dogs tried to lick them, Kit heard a voice. It was like no other voice she'd heard before. It was snuffly and eager and excited. She couldn't tell where it had come from. It definitely wasn't human, she knew that much.

"Mmmm. Goose poo!" it said.

CHAPTER 3

THE VOICES

Kit looked at Josh and Alita. They were staring around, trying to work out where the voice had come from too. Josh knelt down beside the girls.

"What's happening?" he whispered. "Did you both hear that?"

Kit and Alita nodded.

The voice spoke again. "Poo! I found a goose poo! It's mine now! Going to roll in it! Mmmmm! It's so goosey!"

As the voice spoke, the German shepherd rolled on to its back, rocking back and forth on the grass with a look of delight on its furry face. "Stop that!" said the dog walker. "Bad boy!"

Another higher-pitched voice said, "There's a stick. That's my stick! I want that stick!"

"Kit, I think *they're* talking," whispered Alita. She pointed to the tiny Chihuahua, which was now worrying at the sausage dog's stick on the floor.

"Fascinating!" said Josh.

"How is this happening?" asked Kit.

"It has to be magic!" said Alita, gazing around at the talking dogs in wonder.

Meanwhile, the spaniel seemed to be getting annoyed that Alita had stopped stroking it, and put its paw on her knee, licking at her hand.

"More! Human! Friend!" it said. "Give me more strokes!"

Alita blinked. "Sorry," she said, and continued stroking the dog. "They're not just talking. They're talking to *us*!"

The dog walker chuckled. "They do seem like they can talk sometimes," she said.

"I don't think she can hear them talking," Josh

said under his breath. He smiled at the dog walker. "Cute dogs."

"Thanks!" said the dog walker.

"Thanks," said an intelligent-looking collie.

Kit knelt down to stroke it. "Who's a good boy?" she asked, feeling a bit awkward.

"I'm a girl," said the collie. "But I am good. I'm a good girl."

"Why are you talking?" Kit whispered, stroking the collie and leaning close so the dog walker couldn't hear her.

"I'm always talking," said the collie. "It's just that usually no one listens. Can I have some bacon?"

"Pardon?" said Kit.

"Bacon. Since

I have your attention. I'd really like some bacon.
I'm always telling people I want bacon but they
never listen. Bacon?"

"Sorry. No bacon," said Kit, feeling sorry about
disappointing the incredible talking dog.

"I'd better get on," said the dog walker. "Have to
keep up the pace or they all start deciding to wander
off in different directions! Have a nice afternoon!
Lovely day, isn't it?"

"Bye!" said the collie. "Bacon next time?"

The children stared as the dogs trotted away,
chatting as they went.

"Poo again!"

"Bacon!"

"SQUIRREL!"

The children stared after the dogs for a moment.

"What just happened?" said Kit.

"A spell?" suggested Josh. "You didn't do that,
did you, Kit?"

"I haven't learned a spell that makes animals
talk," said Kit. "I would definitely remember

learning that! I'd do it every day!"

"Another wizard then?" suggested Alita. She looked around them. The park was quite full. There were people everywhere – having afternoon picnics, playing Frisbee and walking their dogs. "How do you spot a wizard?"

"Well, according to the book Faith gave me, there are no obvious signs, unless you have special equipment, like a thaumometer," said Josh. "Wizards look just like you and me. Or Kit, obviously."

"Let's walk around – see if we can spot anyone doing spells," said Kit.

They couldn't see anyone who looked like they were doing magic. No one waving their hands suspiciously, or muttering words in the mish-mash of languages that made up magical spells. Not a single wizard anywhere.

But as they passed a flock of crows all clustering round a tree, they heard something.

"Get off my perch, you bunch of scraggly

pigeon-lickers!"

"It's my perch, not yours!" said a second crow. "Get your own perch, you tatty-feathered slow-flapper!"

"Hey, crows!" Alita called up to the tree. "Can you understand us?"

The children heard some whispering and then a
bird flew down and landed on the ground, blinking
up at them with its black eyes.

"We understand you. But we don't know why,"
said the crow. The bird peered up at Kit. "Wizard,"
it said. "I smell wizard. Did you do this?"

"No, I swear," said Kit.

"Humph," said the crow. "It's usually wizards.
Don't trust wizards. Oh! Worm! Crowkind, alert!
Worms!"

The rest of the crows flocked down and started
pecking at the ground, ignoring the children and
feasting on delicious wriggly worms.

Kit, Josh and Alita moved on. As they reached a
wooded part of the park, they heard some squeaking
voices. It took a while to work out where the voices
were coming from, until Alita knelt down and
pointed. "Ants!" she said. "There's a colony living
here."

But although they were saying words in English,
none of it made any sense. Each ant on the ground

would squeak out words, seemingly at random.

"Earth!"

"Magic!"

"A!"

"Change!"

"New!"

"Coming!"

"Beneath!"

"Hungry!"

"Wait," said Alita. "Insects are hive creatures. They do everything as a group. So each ant isn't going to say anything interesting. We need to put it all together. Maybe the order of the words doesn't matter?"

"But I don't think we can hear *all* the ants speaking," objected Josh. "They're spread over too wide an area. So we'd probably miss some words."

"We could go around recording them all?" Alita said. "Then put it together afterwards?"

"Or we could just try to find a creature that makes sense on its own?" suggested Kit. She'd spotted a water vole in the undergrowth by the lake. "Hey!" she called, waving at the vole.

It gave her a distrustful stare.

"No! Not talking to you," said the vole. "Humans own cats. And dogs. Dogs eat voles. Humans are bad news!"

"I promise I won't hurt you!" called Kit. "And I

don't have a dog!"

"But I have food," said Alita, trying a different approach. She pulled out a bag of crisps from her skirt pocket. The vole looked interested.

"I'm listening…" It scuttled closer.

Alita held out her palm with some crisps on. Kit wondered if putting your fingers within biting range of a toothy little mammal was a good idea, but the vole came up quickly and nabbed the crisps from her palm, then scuttled back to a safe distance.

"Why can you talk?" asked Josh, as the vole nibbled.

"Why can YOU talk?" asked the vole. "You can't normally. Just human noises."

"Have you noticed anything weird?" asked Kit. "Like … anyone doing magic spells?"

"Don't know about magic," said the vole. "But there's something…" It glanced around conspiratorially. "Something new here. More crisps?"

Alita shook her head.

"Bye!" said the vole, and disappeared into the undergrowth again.

"The animals in this park are VERY unhelpful," said Josh grumpily.

"I think they're just hungry," said Alita. "I'm not very talkative when I'm hungry."

"It's a pity there aren't any monkeys here. I bet they'd be better at explaining things," said Kit. "Cos they're more like us."

"Crows are actually very intelligent," said Alita. "But I don't think they care much about us and what we want. I wouldn't, if I was them. They're interested in crow things."

"If the animals aren't going to be helpful, how

are we going to work out what's going on?" asked Josh.

"Well, no one else seems to be able to hear the animals talking," said Kit. She gestured to the other people in sight. Everything else seemed normal and no one was running around screaming, "OMG! Talking animals!"

"Maybe it's because we're kids," suggested Josh. "Adults are too close-minded to see stuff they don't expect to see? That's how it is sometimes in Danny Fandango."

"But there are kids here too," said Alita. She pointed to a small boy not far away, playing fetch with a spaniel. There was no sign that they were having a conversation.

"So it's just us who can talk to the animals," said Kit. "That would make sense if it was just me because I'm a wizard but you two can as well so..." She frowned. "How can we find out what's going on?"

Josh and Alita both smiled at once. Kit didn't

like those smiles. "I know," said Josh. "We can go to the library and RESEARCH!"

"Or … I could do a spell?" suggested Kit.

"Or we could research."

"So … we're going to go and sit inside and read books on a day like this?" asked Kit.

"Exactly," said Alita. "Yay! Books!"

"Yay," said Kit, in the least "yay" voice imaginable.

CHAPTER 4

THE LIBRARY

When they arrived at the library they asked Greg, the Assistant Librarian, for help. But when they described what was happening, Greg shrugged, making his long white beard sway. "Talking dogs? Not my problem," he mumbled. "Plus, I'm knocking off in an hour. It's nearly five and I don't want to be starting anything complicated that'll make me late home. The darts is on."

At the best of times Greg was not very helpful. And when Faith was away he was even less helpful, because being in charge of the library alone put him into a foul mood.

"Please, Greg," said Alita. "Are there any books

about this sort of thing? Has it happened before?"

Greg grunted. "Nothing new under the sun. Everything's happened before, one time or another. Try the magical history section in the Stacks."

So the children headed down to the library Stacks, through a bookshelf at the back of the library floor. Kit pulled at one of the books and said the spell that opened the door.

"*Labah!*"

Her fingers glowed, and the entire shelf slid silently aside.

"That never gets less cool," said Josh.

Kit grinned. He wasn't wrong.

"Let's go," she said. "*Ina*," she added, touching her forehead and focusing on the air above her. A magical light appeared, and they walked down the dark, book-lined corridor that led to the Book Wood. The books themselves sat on shelves – further down into the Stacks grew trees that had once been books, with spells carved into their trunks and pages for leaves. But today they were interested in the books in the corridor, which was where the magical history books were kept.

They ended up with more books than they could carry, so Kit had to perform a lifting spell to take some of the weight, which she couldn't manage at the same time as the light spell, so they stumbled out of the corridor in darkness, scuffling and bumping until they emerged at the end into the light of the spellbook trees.

"I love magic and everything, but next time," said Josh, "I'm going to bring a torch."

In the Book Wood, the smell of old paper mingled with a fresh, green smell. Kit smiled. It always gave her a little bubble of joy when she walked down there. A wood beneath a library, where the trees were alive, and magic filled the air.

"Where's Dogon?" asked Alita.

Usually, the little half-dog, half dragon would rush to see Alita, his favourite human, whenever she came down there, but he was nowhere to be seen today.

"Maybe he's sleeping?" said Josh.

"Well, he is half dragon," said Alita. "And they sleep all the time, so that would make sense. But I wish I knew where he was."

They sat in the common room, inside a huge tree in the middle of the forest. Josh had a book on his lap and was reading out passages.

"Apparently animals have started talking without anyone performing spells at different times through history. Usually when something big was going on in the magical world."

"Like what?" asked Kit.

"Like … during a war between wizards," said Josh. "Or when a dragon was waking up."

"Oh!" Alita sat up very straight. Her eyes were wide. "You don't think it could be because Salt nearly woke our dragon?"

Josh thought about this. "Well … maybe. That was a month ago, though, and in this book it said all the weird talking-animal stuff happened at the same time as the dragon waking up."

"Maybe a dragon is waking up now, it's just happening somewhere a bit further away," said Kit. "Should we tell Greg?"

"He didn't seem worried that animals were talking though," said Alita. "And surely he'd know if a dragon was waking up?"

"I suppose so," said Kit, not feeling entirely comforted. Greg never quite seemed in the same world as everyone else, so she wasn't sure if him being calm was a good sign that everything was fine. Kit suspected that Greg's beard could be on fire and it would still take him ten minutes to notice.

"Didn't Faith say the Wizards' Council were being extra cautious at the moment, keeping an eye on all the dragons to make sure none of them were at risk of being woken up?" said Alita. "After what happened with Draca, and Salt nearly waking her up?"

"Maybe we should ask Draca herself what's going on? Whether she's feeling wakeful … or another dragon is," suggested Kit. "I mean, surely dragons know more about dragons than books do!"

"But I've still got ten books I haven't even looked at yet!" complained Josh.

"Well, why don't I go to talk to Draca while you keep reading?" said Kit.

"Mph!" said Josh, who was already deep in the next book. "Good."

"I'll come with you, Kit," said Alita. "I want to ask Draca where Dogon is. It's not like him to hide."

Kit and Alita descended the stairs to the dragon's cave beneath the Book Wood. Kit felt her stomach tighten as she reached the bottom of the staircase. What if the dragon *was* waking up again? The building wasn't shaking at least. That was a good sign. When Salt had nearly woken Draca, the whole building shook, and smoke rose up through the library.

Sure enough, when Kit entered Draca's cave, the dragon was fast asleep. Little puffs of smoke rose out of the nostrils of her long snout, rising up to the high stone ceilings. Kit held out her hand to Alita. "Shall we join her dreams?"

Alita took her hand and grinned. "I could spend days in there," she said. "You know, if it wouldn't drain you of all your power and leave you as limp as a wet sock."

It took a lot of magic to remain in the dragon's dream, especially if you were taking someone who wasn't a wizard in there, so they'd have to be quick.

The two girls knelt beside the dragon, and Kit put one hand on Draca's flank, holding Alita's hand with the other. The dragon was cold to the touch, and the scales were rough, with sharp edges. Kit's fingers began to tingle as the dragon's magic flowed through them.

"Tickles!" murmured Alita, feeling it too.

A rush of heat washed through Kit, then everything went dark.

When the light returned, they were inside the

dragon's dream. Today, Draca was dreaming of a yellow brick road leading to a glistening green castle.

The dragon was sitting in a field of red poppies beside the road, watching them curiously with bright-green eyes. Just then, a monkey flew overhead on feathery wings.

"Friends!" said Draca. "Welcome!" She gestured around with her claws. "Someone read this book in the world above last week. Or years ago. Or now." She shook her head. "Human time is hard for me…"

Kit smiled. She'd been the one to read some of *The Wizard of Oz* in the library for Storytime last week. The book was set in a magical land called Oz, where a wizard lived in a shining green city, and a girl called Dorothy had to journey along a yellow brick road, fighting witches and evil flying monkeys with the help of her friends. The only disappointment for Kit was that Dorothy didn't turn out to be a wizard, although she did have magic shoes, so that was something.

"I'm glad you liked it," said Kit.

"You feed my dreams," said Draca approvingly.

"It's a good story," said Alita. "Though it's not as good as the Danny Fandango books."

Draca's eyes lit up. "Will you read me the new one soon? *Danny Fandango and the Crown of Bones*?" she asked. As the dragon spoke, their surroundings changed. Now they were in a stone room with cross-shaped windows. Draca was curled up on a vast, dragon-sized four-poster bed, and the children were sitting at the foot of it.

"Where are we?" asked Kit.

"Lara Fandango's bedroom from Book Two, in the High Tower, when she and Danny are adopted by a queen! Only her bed isn't usually that big," said Alita.

"It's my dream," said Draca. "Everything is me-sized here."

Draca grinned, showing her shining fangs. No matter how often Kit came to see Draca, she could never quite get used to chatting as friends with a creature that looked like she could eat you in a single chomp.

"I would never eat you, Kit Spencer," said Draca.

Alita laughed. "Don't think bad thoughts around mind-reading dragons, Kit."

"Sorry," blushed Kit. "I forgot."

But Kit's mind wasn't the only one that Draca could read.

The creature turned her scaly head towards Alita. "You are worried about Dogon, aren't you? I'm worried too. The little one has been visiting me in dreams," said Draca.

"You mean, like we are now?" said Alita. "I didn't know he could do that."

"No, when he sleeps, he wanders into my dreams. He's been wandering more lately…"

"You mean, he's been sleeping a lot?" suggested Kit.

"Yes," said Draca. "He came to play with me when I was on a ship, sailing around the world, and when I was with a monkey who set fire to a city full of demons."

"I hope he's not sick," said Alita.

"I'm sorry, but he is," said Draca. "And getting weaker."

"Oh no!" said Alita. She gripped Kit's hand and

Kit gave hers a squeeze back.

"We came to ask something else too," said Kit. "We wanted to check if you were feeling like waking up? Or if you know of anything else funny going on with magic?"

Draca didn't reply at first. Her eyes fixed on the distance, and a little burst of flame rose out of each nostril with a huff, as though she was sighing. Around them, the world shifted. Sparkles of magic filled the air, moving gently at first, then beginning to whirl faster and faster, until Kit felt dizzy.

"There's … something new," said Draca, above the whirl of magic. "It's not above, not in the library. It's beyond. Where things are green and there is water…" She shuddered. "Something is not quite right. Something sad."

"What does that mean?" said Kit.

"Green…" said Alita. She tapped Kit's arm excitedly. "The park! It's something in the park!"

"Someone is there. Someone new. Too much wild. Too strong."

The whirling magic faded around them and was replaced with an image of the dragon's cave. Draca gave out a little roar.

"Are we bothering you?" asked Alita, looking worriedly at Draca. "You're not … waking up are you? If you are going to wake up, please tell me so I can warn my family to get out of town!"

"Waking up? Hmmm… I'm not sure. I think you should go upstairs and read me a story, just in case," said Draca, with a sly grin.

Alita grinned. "Sneaky Draca. But I love you anyway."

"I do think we need to go," said Kit. "I feel … drained." She yawned. Her body was heavy and her mind felt like sludge.

To leave the dragon's dream, all Kit had to do was say goodbye.

"Bye, Draca! See you soon!" she said, and, with a flash of black, they were back beside the sleeping dragon.

Kit felt utterly exhausted, like she'd just run a

mile in lead shoes, carrying her entire family on her
back.

"PHEW!" she said. "I'm not looking forward to
the stairs."

"Want to sit for a bit?" asked Alita.

There was a little stone bench outside the
dragon's cave, and the two girls sat. The stone was
cold against Kit's bare legs.

"What do you think that meant, about the park?"
asked Kit.

"She said there's someone new," said Alita. "A
wizard, maybe? Visiting from somewhere?"

"Maybe. Though Draca said, 'too much wild'.
But wizards don't bring wild magic with them. That
comes from dragons," objected Kit. "And I think
Draca would've mentioned another dragon, if there
was one living under the park."

Alita thought about this. "Yes, wild magic
comes from dragons... but not JUST dragons. Other
magical creatures give off wild magic too."

"They DO?" asked Kit.

"You should read more," said Alita.

Kit groaned. "I don't think I could physically read any more than I do already. I think I have librarian's elbow from turning too many pages."

"That is absolutely not a thing," said Alita.

After a rest, and a very slow climb, they rejoined Josh upstairs in the common room.

"I've found something!" he said, tapping his book and looking up in excitement.

"Us too! Draca was really helpful!" said Alita. "Though she also said Dogon is sick, which is..." She tailed off, biting her lip. "But what did you find?"

"I read that too much wild magic in a single place can cause spontaneous spells, such as – check this out – animals talking! But also..." Josh was pointing to places in his book, then flipping pages faster than a human could possibly read. Or at least faster than Kit could. "Also, also," Josh went on, eyes on fire with excitement. "Too much wild magic in a place can also make wizards' spells go wrong!"

Kit almost yelled with relief. "I *knew* I wasn't getting that fireball spell wrong! It was wild magic, not me!" She started doing a little victory dance. Then she stopped when she realised how sore and tired she was from keeping Alita and herself in Draca's dream. She sat down on a chair, ever so gently.

"What did Draca tell you about what's causing the animals to talk?" asked Josh.

Alita told Josh their theory that there was a magical creature living in the park that shouldn't be there. Not a dragon. Something else.

"Could it be underground?" asked Josh.

"It could be living in a sewer beneath the park," suggested Alita. "Maybe it's a magical rat?"

"That's gross," said Kit. She grinned. "I LOVE IT!"

"I hope it's not a sewer creature though," said Josh. "My mum would kill me if I came home smelling of sewer."

"Speaking of coming home, my mum's expecting me for dinner soon," said Alita.

"Shall we go and search the park tomorrow then?" asked Kit.

The others agreed. "Just wait a few minutes, though," said Alita. "I need to go and look for Dogon. Draca said he's sick, and he's been sleeping a lot, and I know all his favourite places for naps."

Alita came back a few minutes later, holding Dogon in her arms. The furry, puppy-like creature was still half asleep, letting out little drowsy growls. She put him down and he stretched out his red wings and took a few feeble steps.

"Are you OK, Dogon?" She turned to the others. "I found him sleeping beneath a tree. He'd made a nest out of moss."

"Rrrrrrr!" Dogon growled. As though to prove he was fine, he flapped groggily into the air, displaying his scaly green belly. He only made it a little way before he started to sink to the ground, exhausted.

"He's really not himself," said Alita. She knelt down to stroke Dogon. "I think he really is sick!"

Kit and Josh clustered round.

"His scales look sort of ... flaky," said Josh.

"Maybe it's not serious?" said Kit. "Maybe it's just ... like a magical cold?"

"I don't like it," said Alita. "I wish the wild magic was making Dogon talk. Then he could tell us what's wrong." Alita put her hand on Dogon's head and he leaned into it, demanding strokes.

"When Faith comes back, maybe she can take him to a dragon vet?" suggested Kit.

"When *is* Faith coming back?" asked Josh.

"She didn't say. Just that she had a Wizards' Council meeting," said Kit.

Alita carried a sleepy Dogon to a soft patch of moss and laid him down to rest. She looked back at him, frowning. "Should we leave him alone while he's ill?" she said.

"I'm sure he'll be OK," said Kit, trying to sound certain.

CHAPTER 5
WILD MAGIC MAKES THINGS WONKY

Early the next morning, they met up by the
tennis courts to search every inch of the park for
magical creatures. Kit got briefly excited when
she spotted a flash of dark fur in the bushes by the
toilets, but when she followed the creature into the
undergrowth, it just turned out to be a large German
shepherd. It looked at her, panting.

"There was a vole!" it said excitedly. "I think it's
still here!"

"You haven't seen … some kind of magical
creature, have you?" asked Kit.

"Don't know about magical creatures. But there
was a vole!" said the dog. "A big one. I'm going

to eat it! Or make it my friend. I haven't decided.
VOLE!" It put its nose to the ground and snuffled
off through the bushes.

"Anything?" asked Alita, following Kit. Josh
was behind her, peering around for any rogue
monsters that might come leaping out of the bushes.

Kit shook her head. "Just a dog. It was talking,
but it was just a dog."

"So that means whatever the creature is, it's still
around somewhere," said Josh. "If it wasn't, the
talking spell would have worn off by now, wouldn't
it?"

"I don't know where it can be, though," said Kit.
"Maybe it *is* time to try the sewers? How do you
get into sewers, anyway? Maybe one of those metal
covers on the floor? Oh, I know! I learned a spell
to reveal hidden entrances." She lifted one hand
and lowered the other towards the ground, thinking
about the sewers beneath her feet. "*Pradarshan*!"
she said.

A wobbly glowing light appeared, beaming from

the tips of her fingers and pointing towards a metal grate in the floor towards the edge of the lake.

"There!" said Kit in delight. The spell worked! Nothing went wrong! "That's the way into the sewers!"

"Wait," said Alita. "Maybe we don't need to go into the sewers quite yet…"

"Oh good!" said Josh.

Alita pointed to a bush, not far away, growing at the edge of the lake. "Notice anything weird?"

They went closer, and Kit saw that the bush had some leaves missing. It looked as though something had taken a bite out of it.

"It wasn't like that a few minutes ago when we came past," said Alita. "I think whatever it is … is near."

The children instinctively huddled closer together, glancing around.

"I wish Faith was here," said Josh. "She'd know what to do."

"Wish granted," said a voice.

They turned, and there was Faith, standing right behind them. She was holding her arms aloft and her dark eyes sparkled like gems.

"Wait," said Josh. "Do you … do wizards … grant wishes?"

Faith laughed loudly. "HA! No, they just know how to make an entrance." She lowered her arms and her eyes stopped sparkling. "I spotted you three across the park coming out of those bushes. I've been here a couple of minutes. I thought I'd just wait until you noticed me. You really need to work on your observation skills."

Kit went red. "I was distracted. We're looking for a monster…"

"And Dogon's sick!" added Alita. "He's gone all flaky and floppy! Draca said he's getting worse too!"

"A monster? Dogon's ill?" said Faith. She looked serious. "Catch me up."

They filled her in on their hunt for a wild-magic-creating monster in the park, the talking animals, and Dogon's flaky skin and worrying sleeping patterns – plus the fact that they had just found a bush with a bite missing.

"So with all this wild magic washing about, my spell going wrong this morning wasn't my fault." Kit thought it was very important to point that out.

"I see," nodded Faith. "Odd, though. A visiting magical creature could definitely cause animals to talk, and disrupt your spells, but it should settle down in a matter of hours, not last for days." She looked thoughtful. "I'll worry about that in a moment. Go on. What else do you know?"

"Well, we don't know what kind of creature is behind it all, or where it is," added Josh. "But we do know it likes the taste of bushes."

Kit looked at the bush with the bite taken out of it. She looked beyond it. There was another bush with snapped twigs, closer to the water. Something very big had been that way. "I think…" She pointed behind her. "It might be in the lake!"

Faith pulled out her thaumometer and held the object out. Its gems began to glow brighter and brighter. To Kit's surprise, Faith stepped right into the lake. The thaumometer glowed bright red and started to emit a squealing noise like a frightened pig. "Well. That answers that," she said.

CHAPTER 6

THE MONSTER IN THE LAKE

"We need to talk to it, whatever it is," said Faith, after doing a quick spell to dry and clean her dress. "But we can't have all the park listening in. Do you remember the cloaking spell we did last week, Kit?"

Kit tried to think back. "Was that the one that went wrong and I ended up making my face invisible but nothing else, so it looked like I had no face, and Josh was nearly sick?"

"I remember," said Josh with a shudder. "That was so wrong. People should have faces."

"It wasn't even *your* face that went missing!" pointed out Kit. "It was worse for me!"

Josh shook his head in disagreement. "If it *was* my face I wouldn't mind, because I wouldn't be *able* to *not* see it, so it wouldn't be as creepy."

Faith cleared her throat. "Do you think you can do the spell correctly this time, Kit? So that you cloak the area around us and prevent anyone else seeing or hearing anything they shouldn't?"

"Maybe you should do it?" Josh suggested to Faith. "Since Kit's magic is going wonky."

Kit glared at Josh. He might be a genius, but if there was an intelligence test for tact, he'd score minus points.

"She'll be fine," said Faith. "It's not a big spell, and I'm right here to help if she needs it. Kit?"

Kit nodded. She mimed the word and gesture to herself before saying it out loud. In spite of nerves that felt like a bag of fighting cats in her stomach, she took a deep breath and performed the spell. "*Skor!*"

She felt the usual rush that came with any spell and the sunshine dimmed a little. She looked at

Faith, who nodded.

"Good," said Faith. "It worked."

Kit pointed at her face. "All there?"

"All there," said Josh, looking relieved.

"Well done. Now." Faith gestured to the lake. "Let's see who we have here."

"How do we summon … whatever it is?" asked Alita.

"I like to use a little spell I call … yelling," said Faith. "OI!" she shouted. "You in the lake! You know who I mean. Whoever's not meant to be there. Come out! It's safe … but we'd like to talk to you!"

There was a moment's silence, and then the water began to ripple outwards from the centre of the lake, and a dark shape rose to the surface. A smooth little head popped up, about the length and shape of a large dog's snout, but earless, with two beady eyes on either side of the face. It blinked at them.

"How did you know I was here?" it said. It

spoke with an accent. It sounded … Scottish? Kit wasn't very good at accents. The creature raised its head a little further, showing a long neck. It looked around nervously. "We're cloaked, right? I felt the spell…"

"Yes, we're perfectly safe," said Faith. "We only spotted you because you're causing the local wild magic levels to spike." She looked thoughtfully at the creature. Its face was lined with sadness.

The creature bit its lip and looked down into the water. "I'm sorry if I'm causing trouble," it said. "I just don't have anywhere else to go."

"How did you get here?" asked Kit. "Did you come through the sewers?"

The creature made a face. "No. Ew! I came through a water portal. From Scotland."

Kit heard Josh gasp next to her. "Are you … the Loch Ness monster?" he said. "I've read about you!"

"No, I'm not, and no, you haven't!" said the creature, looking displeased. "I'm not fame-seeking! Not like that Nessie." The creature wrinkled its snout. "I'm Lizzie! I'm what's known as a Lesser Nessie by some, though I've always found that insulting. I'm not Lesser. I'm just … more low-key, you know?"

"Oh," said Faith. "I *have* read about you! There's a book in my friend's library in the Highlands about the—" Faith hesitated.

"You were going to say Lesser Nessies, weren't you?" said Lizzie.

"Let's say loch creatures of a more subtle style," said Faith.

A loch is what they call a lake in Scotland.

"Loch creature is right," said Lizzie. "I'm from Loch Lochy."

Kit thought that was a very unimaginative name for a loch. It might as well be called Lochy McLochface.

"So what brought you here?" asked Alita.

"Mermaids," said Lizzie, her mouth turning down and little wrinkles appearing on her slimy forehead. "They kicked me out. Barred me from my own loch. So I came here."

Kit blinked. "Wait, what? Mermaids?" She wasn't so much shocked that mermaids were real, but that they were living in a lake. "I thought mermaids belonged in the sea."

"Some do, some don't," said Lizzie. "Just like fish. You get freshwater mermaids and sea ones. And these particular mermaids ... well. They were never any trouble, until their leader, Morag, got it into her scraggly head to kick me out. She claims the lake is for mermaids only now. She said I had to leave. I'm not a fighter. I like a quiet life, and she's scary when she's angry. So I left and came here."

"Why here?" asked Kit. "It's a long way."

"Portal was open," said Lizzie. She sniffed. "You can't blame me for coming in. You left the door open."

Faith gave a little sharp breath. "Oh."

Kit looked up to her.

"Tell you later," said Faith. "Now, Lizzie, you being here is a problem. It's disrupting the levels of wild magic."

"I could go somewhere else," said Lizzie, looking a bit sad. "Though I was just starting to get comfortable. Some tasty bushes you've got around here…"

"I'm afraid you going to another lake wouldn't solve the issue," said Faith. "I think I can see the problem here. Ordinarily, a magical creature moving home would cause a bit of trouble at first, but only for a few hours, and it certainly wouldn't make magical creatures sick. But you being kicked out of home." She shook her head. "Your sadness has thrown your own wild magic out of whack, making it surge. You're affecting all the creatures around you – magical and non-magical."

"And wizards," added Kit. "Well, me anyway."

"Och, I might as well stay here then," said Lizzie. She blinked her black little eyes and shrugged her flippers. "I can't win. It'll be just as bad somewhere else, won't it? Because I'll be just as sad."

"You can't stay here, I'm afraid," said Faith. "We've been having some issues with talking dogs."

"And insects. And rodents," pointed out Josh. "And birds," he added.

"Is that bad?" asked Kit. "No one else noticed but us. Why DID no one else notice?" she asked Faith.

"You've spent time around the dragon – you, Alita and Josh – not to mention read a lot of magical books. And you're a wizard, Kit ... so." Faith gestured around her at the park. "You're all able to see things other people can't."

The children exchanged pleased glances.

"We're like those dogs that can smell explosives!" beamed Josh.

When Kit and Alita gave him funny looks, he added, "That sounded cooler in my head."

"Well," said Lizzie. "Since only these ... unusual children can see me, I don't see why I can't just stay here." She sniffed. "A few talking dogs that only you people can hear won't do anyone any harm."

"Not yet," said Faith. "But if you stay much longer

here, your magic would affect things more, and eventually we'd have *everyone* noticing magic. And we all remember what happened last time a powerful person found out about magic." Faith gave a pointed look at the children.

"I don't," said Lizzie.

"There was a man called Salt who found out about magic and tried to wake the dragon and it was bad," explained Josh. "I have the longer version written down in my notes if you'd like to read?"

Lizzie blinked her little eyes in surprise. Her mouth opened and shut again. "Oh no! A woken dragon!"

"Semi-woken," corrected Josh.

"We got her to sleep again," added Alita.

"Well, that'll explain why your water portal was open," said Lizzie.

The children turned to Faith questioningly.

"I'll explain later," said Faith.

Lizzie shook her head. "Well, I don't like to be any bother, but I don't know what to do. I can't go back while the mermaids won't let me … and they've started peeing at my end of the loch." Lizzie shuddered. "And they've threatened worse if I come back."

"But if you stay your wild magic will do all kinds of damage," said Faith.

Alita gave a little gasp. "I think it already is. Could that be what's making Dogon sick?"

Faith frowned. "Oh. I hadn't thought of that. Yes. It might just be that."

"Sorry about your dog," said Lizzie. "Can't help you, though. I'm too scared to go back." She began to sink.

"Wait," said Kit. "We can talk to the mermaids for you. Maybe we can get them to change their minds?"

"Be my guest," said Lizzie. "But don't get too close. Remember, they pinch … and bite. And pee!"

With that, she sank beneath the surface of the lake.

They walked back to the library, all feeling glum. Faith explained all about water portals, and Josh was scribbling notes as he walked, which meant he bumped into a lamp post halfway back.

So, water portals connect lakes and streams and other bits of water all over the world together, using magic. All water is connected, and you could have a portal from anywhere to anywhere in theory, but someone has to open them. If they were open all the time, you'd end up with magical creatures in swimming pools or even your bath, and that would be freaky.

When Salt nearly woke Draca, that opened the water portal here to the one where Lizzie is from. Faith says it should close naturally in a day or so.

They gathered in the scruffy, cosy common room

in the Book Wood beneath the library. Alita had Dogon on her lap. He was trembling, and had snuggled into her like a baby.

"We can't leave him here," said Alita.

"I'm afraid you're right. He'll only get sicker while Lizzie is here," said Faith. She came over and knelt next to Dogon, giving him a stroke. "Her unstable, sad wild magic is really bad for him."

"Oh no!" said Alita. "Poor Dogon!"

"I think we should take him away from here until we can persuade Lizzie to leave," said Faith.

"Can't we just cheer her up?" suggested Kit.

Faith shook her head. "I'm afraid nothing will cheer her up except being allowed home again. Magical creatures can be very attached to the places they come from. They're not very adaptable. That's what happens when you're millions of years old."

"But if we take Dogon away … won't it be bad if we take him away from the dragon?" asked Alita. "Isn't that the source of his magic?"

"Not if we're not away too long," said Faith.

"He's got enough dragon magic in him to keep him healthy and happy for at least a week away from Draca."

"Wait, a *week*?" said Josh, looking alarmed. "Where are we going? What will I tell my mum? I'm supposed to be back in time for dinner at six tonight! In eight hours' time! If I'm away a second longer, my mum will flip! My dad will BACKFLIP!"

"Easy, no one's going away for a week," said Faith. "I'm hoping we can get all this wrapped up long before your families even start worrying about where you are."

"My ma worries even when I'm *with* her," said Alita, with a half-smile. "But as long as we're back for dinner, she'll keep her worrying to her normal speaking voice, not her shouting voice."

"Where *are* we going?" asked Kit, whose own parents probably wouldn't notice if she was several days late for dinner.

"Well, I was thinking we should go to Scotland to investigate the loch. How does that sound?" asked

Faith.

Kit thought it sounded excellent. "I've never been to Scotland!" she said.

"You'll like it. It's very … outdoors," said Faith with a smile.

"How will we get there?" asked Alita. "I don't think my parents would let me take a train on my own. Even with you, Faith," she added apologetically. "And wouldn't that be expensive?"

"We won't be going by train. We'll be going by book!" said Faith.

"A portal book?" asked Kit excitedly. These were the special books used by wizards to travel between libraries. Each book took you through a different landscape on your way, depending on what the book was about. Some of them were safer to cross than others…

"So what library will we be going to?" asked Alita, focusing on entirely the wrong part of their journey, as far as Kit was concerned.

"Invergloy," said Faith. "It's near the loch where

the mermaids live, Loch Lochy."

"Are there libraries by lochs? Like, in the middle of nowhere?" asked Josh, wide-eyed.

"Sort of," said Faith. "You'll see when we get there."

"Can we take Dogon to Scotland with us?" asked Alita. She hugged the little furry dragon creature tight.

"Yes, definitely," said Faith. "He should start feeling better as soon as he's away from Lizzie." She got up and went to a cupboard underneath the sink. "I think his carrying case should be under here. Usually I'd let him fly but the poor thing can barely flap right now. Hmmm..." She pulled out a bottle of some kind of glowing liquid, a pair of high-heeled shoes, a tin of paint with a label reading "Hex-Resistant Pixie House Paint" and a small statue of an octopus with what looked like diamonds for eyes, until she found what she was looking for. "Bring him over here."

Alita carried Dogon over and put him in the

carrying case, which was bright red and hovered just above the ground.

"I could do with one of those for my school books," said Josh, impressed. "How does it work?"

"A fairly simple levitation spell, kept going by crystals in the base of the case," said Faith. "The crystals act like batteries for magic, you see."

"Cool!" said Josh, scribbling notes in his little book.

Alita gently encouraged Dogon inside the case. He made a grumpy sound, but was too tired to resist.

"Right. Let's get him out of here," said Faith. "I'll just call ahead to let the librarian know we're coming. Would you get a portal book? Invergloy has all the same ones as us apart from *Dangerous Animals*."

"Good," said Josh. "That one's terrifying."

Kit went to the shelf where the portal books sat and unlocked it with the spell Faith had taught her. She picked one she hadn't used before, called

Inside a Computer. It was a large book, with bright pictures and flaps to lift.

When Faith came back from calling the Invergloy librarian, they were ready to go. Kit started reading the book.

"Computers are like libraries, but instead of books, they store information using 0s and 1s..."

They found themselves inside the book. It wasn't like some of the other portal books, where you walked through a realistic landscape. In here, lines of light surrounded them, forming a sort of cage. Beeping sounds filled the air. Kit saw some moving platforms ahead, and old-fashioned robots bustling around looking busy.

"Is this what a computer looks like inside?" asked Alita doubtfully.

"No, this is how Kit imagines it would look," said Faith.

"It looks like a computer game!" said Josh.

"Well, that's what you find inside any good computer," said Kit. "Which way do we go?" she asked Faith.

Faith pointed to the moving platforms. "That way. We'll have to jump a bit. Dogon's case will just float behind us."

They started to make their way through the book, hopping from platform to platform. It wasn't too hard. In fact, Kit loved it. She made a mental note to use this book as often as possible when they travelled between libraries. It was safer than the *Dangerous Animals* portal book, but a lot more fun than the *Garden* one.

When they got to the end of the moving platforms, they walked through a shining door made from light. The next page of the book was a room with green walls and a green floor, all covered in silver metal wires.

"It's a circuit board!" said Josh.

The next room was full of ancient computers, covered in dust.

"This is the page about the history of computing," said Faith.

"Oh, I think my nan has that one," said Kit, pointing to a big, box-like computer.

One of the machines didn't even look like a computer – it had a hand crank to one side, and lots of what looked like metal cogs.

"Oh wow! A difference engine!" said Josh. "It's an early version of a computer! From hundreds of years ago!"

"Sometimes I wonder if there's ANYTHING you don't know," said Kit.

"I don't know the rules of baseball," said Josh, after a moment's thought. "I should learn them soon!"

The next room was full of robots. Some were just arms, building and painting a car. Kit could smell the fresh paint. It made her feel giddy. Another was playing football with itself.

"This one looks almost human!" said Kit, marvelling at a robot with skin that looked surprisingly realistic.

"Thank you," said the robot. It was dressed as a butler and had a moustache. "How may I be of service?"

"Can I have some toast?" asked Kit.

The robot pressed its stomach and out popped hot buttered toast.

Kit had to be dragged out of that room, clutching two wedges of perfectly browned bread.

"Come on," said Faith. "Remember what happens if you stay in one spot in a portal book?"

Kit did. You risked going into a trance and if you stayed too long … you might not be quite right again once you returned to the real world.

"What happens if you DIE in a portal book?" asked Kit, about to take a bite of her toast.

"It's best to avoid it," said Faith. She pointed at Kit's toast. "And I wouldn't eat *that* either."

Kit dropped the toast hastily. As it hit the ground, it

disappeared in a cloud of square pixels. Kit gulped.

"I bet eating THAT would've given you indigestion," said Josh, watching the toast pixels as they floated away.

After a few more pages, they reached the end of the book – a vast wall of screens, flashing images showing people going about their business – including one group of men who Kit thought were almost definitely robbing a bank.

"Don't worry. It's not real," said Faith. "All part of the book."

Kit could never get over how real portal books felt when you were in them.

"What's the library called, where we're going?" asked Alita. "This is the end of the book, right?"

"Yes, it's a really short book," said Josh sadly.

"The library's called Invergloy," said Faith.

"*Invergloy, hus!*" said Kit.

They appeared inside what seemed to be a metal container, about the size of Kit's living room at home. A strip light glared down on them from the ceiling. The walls of the box were lined with books, and there was a window at one end, through which Kit could see … seats?

"Oh! We're inside a lorry," said Kit, making sense of the space at last.

"It's a mobile library," said Faith.

There was a clanging sound, doors opened and natural light streamed in through the back of the van. The sky outside was gloomy. A man was looking up at Kit suspiciously. "What are you doing in there?"

He had a big black beard and curly black hair, pale white skin and very arched eyebrows. His clothes were dark and scruffy, and he wore shorts and big walking boots. When he saw Faith, his expression cleared and he gave a huge, welcoming grin. "Ah! It's you! I didn't know you'd be here so soon."

"Hello, Duncan," said Faith. She held up Dogon's carrying case. "We were in a hurry. We had to get this little one clear of… Well, I'll tell you all

that later."

"Who're the bairns?" He peered into the van.

"I'm Kit," said Kit. "This is Josh and Alita. Thanks for letting us come through your … library."

"Sure. Well, come on out, hot day like this, you'll be baking in that van." Duncan gestured out at the rolling moorland behind him.

"It's not hot," said Josh. He peered out of the van at the grey sky. He shivered ever so slightly in his T-shirt.

"Around here, this is beach weather," said Duncan. He held out his hand and helped the children down. "Welcome to Invergloy Mobile Library."

Kit looked around. They were standing on a sloping, wide-open landscape, covered in scrubby plants and dotted with rocks. The lorry was parked on a dirt road. The air smelled fresh.

"Who uses this library?" asked Kit. She couldn't spot anything but grass and little purple plants. "I can't see anyone around."

"I drive around all the local villages so people can borrow books. Plus, I run a festival every summer. People come from all around to listen to stories. But I was on my way home just now. I only parked up to collect some supplies." He gestured to a pile of freshly picked plants.

"Are they for spells?" asked Josh, looking excited.

"Well, that one is … and that one," said Duncan, pointing to a couple of different shrubs. "But that one's for my lunch. Wild rosemary grows around here."

"Sounds delicious," said Faith. "When we've done what we came to do, perhaps you could make us some food?" She grinned, looking to Kit and the others. "Duncan's an EXCELLENT cook."

"And an all right wizard," added Duncan. He waggled his fingers. "Well, I'm no Faith but..."

Faith didn't contradict him.

"So how can I help you?" asked Duncan. "You mentioned Loch Lochy in your message."

"Message?" Kit had a thought. "Can you get a mobile signal out here?"

Duncan shook his head. "Nope. No signal out here at all. But we wizards don't need phones to send messages, do we?"

"Nope." Faith pulled a small, globe-shaped stone out of her pocket, about the size of a golf ball. It was a milky, swirling colour, as if someone had poured white paint into water. It seemed to be glowing from within, giving off pulses of light, as if it was alive.

"Wow! What is it?" asked Kit.

"Wizards call it a duradar. But most people would probably call it a crystal ball," said Faith.

"Can it see the future?" asked Josh.

"Not unless the future is 'you're about to have a cup of tea that you've just asked a wizard friend to put on for you when you arrive'," said Duncan. "It's basically just a wizard phone."

Josh looked a little disappointed.

"On the plus side, it has GREAT reception

absolutely everywhere, and you never need to top up the credit," said Faith. She held out the globe for them all to take a look. Kit took it in her hands. It vibrated ever so slightly, making her skin tingle. She wondered if she'd ever get one of her own.

"Can you point us in the direction of the loch, Duncan?" continued Faith. "Maybe give us an introduction to the mermaids?"

"Yes to directions. It's that way." He pointed at the path behind his lorry. "But I can't introduce you, sorry. I'm nae going near those mermaids again in a hurry. They spat at me last time I went by. And threw a rock at my head!"

"They sound like fun," said Faith, pursing her lips.

"They weren't always like that. They've always been very private people, and a bit grumpy. But they were never aggressive before, and they always lived in peace with the other loch creatures. I don't know what's got into them." He shook his head. "But I went fishing down at the loch the other day.

I'd asked their permission the week before, and
they'd been fine and suddenly…" He shrugged.
"Well. I won't be going back in a hurry."

Kit thought these mermaids sounded much
more interesting than the drippy creatures she'd
read about in fairy tales, who seemed to spend their
time pining after princes and sitting about on rocks
brushing their hair.

"Let's go and meet them!" said Kit.

"Agreed," said Faith. "But I think we should
leave Dogon with Duncan – if you don't mind? Just
in case he bothers the mermaids even more. We
don't want him weeing at the edge of their lake and
starting something."

"Nae bother," said Duncan. "I love dogs." He
peered into the carrying case and raised an eyebrow.
"Or dragons? Anyhoo, I love both."

"Good," said Alita. "Because Dogon IS both."

"What does he eat?"

"Everything," said Alita. "Except mushrooms.
He hates those."

"I'll take him back to my place for some food," said Duncan.

Duncan gave a wave and hopped into the cab of the lorry, gently laying Dogon's carrying case on the seat.

They set off walking towards the loch.

CHAPTER 7
MORAG THE MERMAID

The loch was beautifully still and surrounded by rolling hills. The skies were clearing a little, and while it wasn't sunny yet, there were glimmers behind the clouds. Faith and the children were standing on a pebbly shore.

"How do we get the mermaids to come and talk to us? Do we yell, like with Lizzie?" asked Kit.

Faith shook her head. "I think we need a gentler approach. Mermaids love music. Especially singing."

Kit frowned. "I don't think I should sing. Not unless we want to make them furious."

"Josh can sing," said Alita. "He's in a church choir."

"What should I sing, though?" asked Josh. "What kind of songs do mermaids like?"

"Anything sad," said Faith. "But nothing mentioning sharks. Or fishermen."

In the end, Josh chose a song they'd learned at school, about an octopus. He had a nice voice, Kit thought. Quiet, but sweet.

Nothing happened for a moment. Then, ever so slowly, the surface of the loch began to ripple. Four figures rose up from the dark water, with bare, scaly chests, their seal-like lower halves disappearing into the dark water. The mermaids had tangled hair that, Kit realised, was made of weeds. Their faces were covered in greeny-blue scales, and their eyes were huge and pale, with black slits for pupils. Kit noticed little lines down the side of their necks.

"Ooh – gills!" whispered Alita. "They have gills!" She craned her neck to try to get a better look at the mermaids.

"And I think that one's a boy!" said Josh, pointing to one of the mermaids, who had shorter

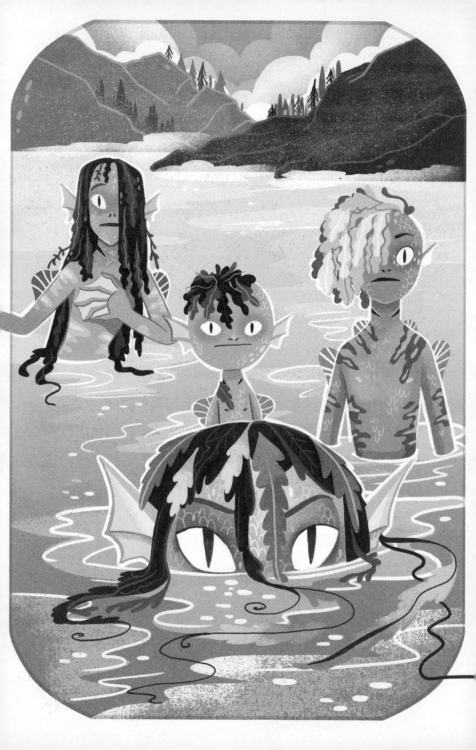

hair and a hint of damp moss around his chin.

"Who disturbs our loch?" said the largest mermaid. Her voice was high and bubbling.

Faith stepped forward. "I am Faith Braithwaite, Wizard of London, Keeper of the Library, My Lady," she said. "We are here to request an audience."

"Why are you talking like that?" whispered Kit.

"It's how mermaids like to be spoken to," whispered Josh. "Shh."

"How does everyone know about mermaids and I don't?" asked Kit.

"Books," said Josh. "Shh."

"Well," said the mermaid. "Faith of London, I am Morag of the Loch. Wizards are not welcome here. This loch is only for us now. No Lesser Nessies, no wizards, no mortals, just my merfolk."

"And fish," added one of the other mermaids.

"Yes," said Morag in a haughty voice. "And fish."

"Why don't you want to share the loch? You

have done for centuries." Faith's voice was perfectly even, but there was a hint of irritation underneath it.

"Things have changed. The world is changing," said Morag. "It's mermaids for mermaids now. We can't allow others to pollute our waters. We want to be left alone."

She opened her pale eyes wider. When she spoke next, her voice took on a strange tone. Kit felt the sound deep inside her chest. It hurt. Part of her wanted to turn and run.

"Go!" said the mermaid.

Kit turned to the others. They looked like they wanted to be sick. Josh took a step back. Alita was bent over, hands on her knees. Faith stood firm, but a flicker crossed her face.

Morag was staring at them. "Why aren't you leaving? I used my Tone of Power! You should be gone by now!"

"Well, here we still are," said Faith. "And, since you're being so rude, I won't bother addressing you in the way you like. It seems your powers are fading.

Don't you wonder why we can approach your lake at all? Why we can see you? You should be able to hide yourselves when you don't want to be seen. Isn't that the mermaid way?"

"Wizard trickery!" spat Morag. But she didn't look entirely certain.

Faith went on. Her voice was level but steely. "Will you allow Lizzie to return? She's causing great harm where she is now with her sadness. She belongs here, with you."

"NO!" shrieked Morag. "Merfolk only!"

"Loch Lochy for the merfolk!" responded the others in a sing-song chorus. "Merfolk! Merfolk!"

"HUMANS OUT! HUMANS OUT!" they all began to chant.

"Well," said Faith. "I don't think we're going to have a sensible conversation here. Let's go. We can think of something else."

"YEAH, YOU'D BETTER RUN!" Morag shrieked after them. "Run on your weird flesh spikes, landscuttlers!"

They walked, rather than running away from the merfolk, but waited until they were a good distance before they started talking.

"Wow. They were MEAN!" said Josh. "And my legs might be skinny, but flesh spikes is a bit harsh!"

"They're *really* mean," agreed Kit. "I can see why Lizzie doesn't want to go back home."

"I want to know more about them, though," said Alita. She turned to Faith. "What do they look like on the bottom half? How can they talk if they have gills instead of lungs? Or do they have both?"

"What's their hair made of?" asked Josh.

"And what was that about them having a Tone of Power?" added Alita.

"And why isn't it working?" asked Josh.

"Honestly?" said Faith. "I'm embarrassed to say I haven't taken the time to study freshwater merfolk in detail, so I don't know as much as I'd like. At the Wizard Academy we mostly focused on the sea-dwelling kind, as they're in the majority all over the world. We'll have to do some more research," she added.

"You mean, we *get* to do more research," corrected Josh.

Kit stifled a groan.

"I have a few answers, though. They *do* have gills and no lungs, I know that," said Faith. "And their hair is ... a kind of underwater moss, I believe. They speak by vibrating certain small bones inside their neck. It's what gives their speech that weird shrill tone. Their Tone of Power is connected to that ... and to their particular type of magic."

If that was what Faith called not knowing anything about a topic, Kit thought, she could fill nine hundred books with the topics she DID know well.

"Duncan will be able to fill us in a little, but yes, we will need to read up more." She gave Josh an indulgent smile.

"Yay!" said Josh.

Faith pulled the duradar out from her pocket. Its

glow increased as she held it, swirling and whirling with milky light.

Faith held the ball up, close to her face, and spoke a one-word spell: "*Parrhesia!*"

The ball flickered from milky-white to a darker colour. A picture was forming, of a shady room full of books, and then Duncan's face came into view.

"Cool!" said Josh. He'd clearly forgiven the ball for not telling the future.

"Hello. Done already?" Duncan asked. His voice was perfectly clear, as though he was standing right next to them.

"Yes, and no luck," said Faith. "The mermaids were more or less how you found them last time. Though they didn't throw any rocks at least."

"Ah, I'm sorry they wouldn't help," said Duncan. "Though you'll be pleased to hear that Dogon has started to perk up, poor wee thing."

Alita gave a happy noise.

"Wait there a sec, I'll come and pick you up," said Duncan, and the duradar went dark.

They didn't have
to wait long before
Duncan's mobile
library appeared
over the nearest
slope. It gave
off no fumes as
it drove along. Kit
wondered if it was
magic.

"Hop in!" called Duncan through the window.
"The back doors of the van are unlocked."

Alita was peering through the window of the
van's cab. "Is Dogon in there with you?"

Duncan shook his head. "He's back at the house.
Want to come and see how he's doing?"

Alita ran to the back of the van and was inside
before he'd finished speaking.

CHAPTER 8

THE WIZARD-HOLE

In the distance, they saw a hill. At least, it looked like a hill, but when Duncan drove them closer, Kit saw there was a large round green door in it.

Hills don't have doors, thought Kit.

"It looks like a hobbit hole!" gasped Alita.

"In a hole in the ground there lived … a wizard," said Duncan.

Duncan pulled open the door, pausing on the doorstep and gesturing to the hill above it. "Having my home underground is very efficient in terms of keeping it heated. There are solar panels over the other side of the hill, and a wee wind farm." He pointed to the ground, where there was a little patch of concrete with a little nozzle poking out of it. "That's where I charge the van when I'm at home."

"Ohhh, is the van electric? I thought it was magic," said Kit. She felt a bit disappointed.

"Powering a van by magic? That sounds exhausting! Do you know how much those things weigh?" said Duncan. "Now, come inside."

The home under the hill was very cosy. The ceiling was only a little taller than Duncan, and even Faith, who was quite a bit shorter than him, had to duck to go through the circular door. The walls were covered with shelves, and every inch of the room seemed filled with furniture. Just then Dogon came barrelling into the main living room from a back room, flying right into Alita and almost knocking her – and a shelf full of knick-knacks – over. While he settled on to her shoulder, Alita stroked his fur and murmured relief into her ears. "You're OK!" she whispered.

Dogon did indeed look much healthier and was clearly full of energy. He spent some of that energy trying to lick every inch of Alita's face with his little forked tongue. She held him at arm's length, giggling as his tongue lapped against empty air. "Sit!" she commanded, as she got over her giggle fit. Dogon fluttered to the floor and took a seat on a rug, looking up expectantly at Alita. "Good boy!" she said approvingly.

"Well, it seems that being away from Lizzie has done him good," said Faith. "Thanks for looking after him, Duncan."

"Nae bother," said Duncan. "He's a very pleasant little house guest, as long you do a few fireproofing spells." He glanced at a singe mark on one of the curtains hanging around the round windows.

Faith sighed. "Sorry about that," she said. She raised a hand and muttered, "*Llosgi no, come back to before.*" With a flick of her wrist, the curtains were as good as new.

Kit made a mental note to use that one. It would come in very handy with toast.

"Ta!" said Duncan. "But, honestly, I've done worse while experimenting with solar energy spells. In fact, this is the third house like this I've built. There's been some trial and error, let's say. With about as many errors as there were trials."

"You burned your house down?" said Josh, looking worried.

"Twice," said Duncan.

"That's so cool!" said Kit.

Faith gave her a look.

"I mean … that's bad. I don't approve," corrected Kit.

As they settled down to make a plan, Duncan brought an apple pie out of the oven. "Brain food," he explained.

"We ARE in a hobbit-hole," said Josh approvingly. "It's like we're having second breakfast!"

Kit didn't know what second breakfast was, but she liked the sound of it. Homemade apple pie at eleven in the morning sounded even better.

It smelled of cinnamon and the hot, crusty pastry looked perfectly done.

"It smells so good!" said Alita.

Dogon immediately flew over to bother Duncan as he dished out the pie, until Alita whistled, and the little dragon dog retreated obediently to her side.

"That's better," she said, nestling Dogon into the gap between her legs and the side of the armchair.

The pie was delicious – sweet and hot, with a dollop of cream on top.

Whether it was the pie, or the warmth of the snug little house, Kit started to feel very sleepy. The others chattered about magical creatures, and apple pie, and Dogon's naughty behaviour as he begged for crumbs.

Kit's mind drifted. She thought about the mermaids, and their angry faces, and Morag's high voice. She thought about Dogon, and how relieved she was that he was looking much better. She thought about the dark water of the loch.

Rising up through the water in her mind's eye,

she saw a horrible face – no, a skull. A tiny, pointed skull, staring up at her from beneath the water. In the sockets of the skull glowed eerily blue eyes. She heard a voice saying, *Let us in.*

A skeletal rat leaped out at her from the water, right at her face, and she let out a silent scream.

She sat up with a start. There was a growling sound beside her.

"You were snoring," said a voice. It was Alita. "I don't think Dogon liked it much." She realised she was slumped forward on her arms, over the table. She sat up, blinking. Dogon gave a disapproving snuffle.

"Sorry," she murmured.

"We didn't like to wake you. You looked so peaceful," said Faith. "At least, until the end."

"Bad dream," muttered Kit.

"You've got apple pie in your hair," pointed out Josh.

Faith gave Kit a look of concern. "Is everything OK?"

Kit shrugged. "Just a bit sleepy."

Faith squinted at her. "If you're sure … then let's do some research. Find out more about what makes these mermaids tick."

Kit couldn't kick the feeling that something was watching her, though. Something with a pointed face and eyes of glassy blue. She thought that she could hear the clattering of bones.

The three children were nestled among gigantic piles of books on cushions in Duncan's little living room. Everyone was sitting in silence – even Dogon was calm, snoozing on a blanket in the corner.

Kit was staring listlessly at her book. She kept trying to focus on the pages, but the words seemed to spin in front of her eyes. She didn't feel very well.

Her book was called *Mermaids: A Beginner's Guide*. But even that seemed too hard. She kept rereading the same passage about scales and gills.

Faith was sitting in a big armchair, reading a large volume called *Beyond the Mermaid: Water Peoples of the World*.

"Apparently, sea merfolk are sometimes known as saltfolk," she was telling them. "Freshwater merfolk, though—"

"Are they called freshfolk?" finished Josh.

"Don't interrupt," said Faith. She tapped the page. "Freshwater mermaids are all named after their individual bodies of water. So, riverfolk, lakefolk and, in the case of Morag and the others, lochfolk. Although they often use 'mermaids' to mean any water people."

Josh scribbled some notes down about this. "What about streams? Are there streamfolk?"

"No, the water's too shallow," said Faith. "But

there are quite a few groups of underwater lakefolk, especially in Mexico. The Cenogente."

Kit r*eally* wasn't feeling well now. Her vision was cloudy and she had a churning feeling in her brain. She could feel tingles in her hands.

"I feel…" she began, but she couldn't finish before–

FWOOM!

Lightning filled the room. Kit took a moment to realise that it was coming from her. Light was streaming from her fingertips. And…

FWOOM!

Suddenly she couldn't see.

"What's happening?" she gasped.

"Your eyes!" cried Alita. "They're … like lasers!"

Kit felt cool hands cupping the back of her

head. Faith's voice spoke a few words: "*Ruo onwe gi!*"

Kit's vision returned, clear as ever. She noticed that the table on the other side of the room was smoking slightly. There was a large scorch mark in the middle.

"Oops," she said. "Sorry!"

Faith was peering at her, worried. "Are you OK?"

"I think … yes. Nothing hurts." She looked at her hands. "What *was* that?"

Alita and Josh rushed to her, looking her over, checking for injuries – and for laser eyes.

"Are you sure you're OK?" asked Alita.

Kit nodded. "What happened?" she asked.

"That was raw wild magic, bursting out of you," said Faith. She frowned. "I've only seen that once, at the Wizard Academy. It happened to a friend of mine during a very difficult spell. I didn't know it could happen spontaneously."

"I'm sorry about the table," was all Kit could

think of to say. She realised she was shaking. She'd never thought of herself as dangerous before. She looked at Alita and Josh. *What if this happens again and I hurt them?*

Alita and Josh were eyeing her cautiously. *Were they afraid of her now?* Well, perhaps they should be.

"What's wrong with her?" asked Josh. "Why did her magic burst out like that?"

The two children hovered around Kit, asking questions. She wanted to snap at them to go away and to stay well away from her, in case she went all laser eyes again. Clearly, Duncan could tell she was worried.

"You've had a real shock. I'll make tea," he said tactfully. "Alita, Josh, can I have a hand with the biscuits? Biscuits are good for shock."

"But I want to know what's going on," said Josh.

"They're VERY heavy biscuits," said Duncan, and led Josh and Alita to the kitchen.

Faith looked Kit in the eye. "Now. Let's see what's up." She pulled out her thaumometer and ran it up and down Kit. It lit up and let out a high-pitched noise that made Kit cover her ears. Faith pulled the thaumometer away, and the noise stopped.

"What's going on?" asked Kit. She felt her heart tha-thumping in her chest. "What's wrong with me?"

"Your wild magic levels are higher than the thaum can measure." Faith frowned so hard her eyebrows almost touched.

"I don't understand," said Kit. "I'm not near Lizzie now. Why is it getting worse? Dogon started going back to normal as soon as he was away from Lizzie."

"I don't know what's happening," said Faith. "But this isn't the same as Lizzie's magic. It's something new. Still," she brightened, "the spell I did to you just now should stop the magic bursting out when you're just sitting there. So there's no immediate danger."

"Right," said Kit. Her voice was small and quiet. Knowing that her magic was out of control felt a little like having an extra limb that could move without her asking it to. Like having a big, swishy tail that smashed things every time she turned round. She didn't like it at all.

"Until we know what's causing this, you'd better be careful while doing magic," said Faith. "If you start feeling odd while doing a spell, stop whatever you're doing right away."

"So I don't have to stop doing magic while I'm like this?" said Kit.

"If I told you to stop doing spells, would you?" Faith raised an eyebrow.

Kit looked away. "Er…"

"I'd rather be realistic." Faith gave her an intense look. "Do magic, but take care."

Just at that moment, they heard Josh let out a yell of shock from the next room. "It's on my feet!"

Alita let out a shriek of delight. "It's so cute! Look at it run!"

"Don't worry," came Duncan's voice. "It's just a rat."

"Just a RAT? JUST a RAT? On my actual feet?"

Josh was yelling now.

"Rat?" Kit's antennae pricked up. "Where?"

Duncan and the others came back into the sitting room. "It's gone now. Fast little thing," said Duncan. "I think it was attracted by the smell of biscuits."

He was carrying two trays – one with a teapot and some cups, the other piled with biscuits.

"Made them myself," said Duncan. "The biscuits, I mean. Not the rat. That arrived of its own accord."

Rats, thought Kit. *Where had she just seen rats?* She tried to grasp at the memory, but it scuttled away into the back of her brain where she couldn't reach it.

"Duncan showed me the oven where he made the biscuits," said Alita. "It's really cool. It's built down into the ground, and he's done a spell to tap into the earth's heat, so it doesn't use much energy."

"Can we do that back at the library?" asked Josh.

"Hmm," said Faith. "I think that the council might have words if I start drilling holes to the earth's core."

When they finished their tea and biscuits, they

went back to their books.

"Oh!" said Alita, who was reading a book called *Deep Sea, Cold Loch: Wild Water Magic*. It was almost as big as she was, and her thin brown arms were clearly straining to keep the book upright as she held it. "This says that saltfolk draw their magic from the sea around them, but also from deep-sea monsters called…" She squinted at an unfamiliar word. "Krakens. Crack-ens? Krarrr-kens?"

"Crack-ens. Of course!" said Faith. Her eyes lit up. "Why didn't I make the connection?" She shook her head. "I sometimes think I've forgotten more than most people learn in a lifetime. Wizards draw their power from dragons. Seafolk draw their power from krakens, so, obviously—"

"Lochfolk get theirs from Nessies!" said Alita and Josh at once.

"Oh, yeah. Obviously…" Kit was feeling sulky and left out. *Why doesn't my brain work fast like theirs do? Instead my brain just shoots out lasers and burns stuff.* She realised Faith was looking at her and tried to put on a more cheerful expression. "So what do we do now?"

"We just need to tell the lochfolk that Lizzie being away is the reason they're losing their powers," said Alita. "Then they'll let Lizzie come home!"

"Wouldn't they know that already?" said Josh. "Like … you know that wizards get their powers from dragons?"

"Not necessarily," said Faith. "Wizards read. Mermaids don't."

"I suppose books *would* get soggy in a loch," said Josh.

"So let's go and tell them that they need to let Lizzie come back," said Kit.

CHAPTER 9

THE QUIET VOICE

The mermaids rose out of the water at the sound of footsteps. Their scaly shoulders and knotty, weed-like hair glistened. Their huge eyes stared. Morag swam to the front of the group, keeping her head above water to keep her gaze fixed on Kit and her friends. Faith stood behind the children, arms folded, observing.

"What do you want?" demanded Morag. "I've told you, you can't bring your pet back here."

"She's not our pet," said Alita. "She's Lizzie."

"Well, she's not welcome," said Morag. "This is OUR loch, and it's going to stay that way."

"It's her loch too!" said Alita.

"Also," said Kit, "aren't you wondering how we found you here? How we can see you?"

"Yeah," said Josh. "I bet you're trying to do your spells to push us away and keep yourself hidden, even now. But they're not working, are they?"

Morag frowned, wrinkling the scales of her forehead. "What would you know about magic, human child?"

"A lot," said Josh truthfully.

Alita was walking down to the bank of the loch.

"Get back!" said Morag. "You can't touch our water!"

Alita pulled off her shoe and sock and neatly dipped a toe in the water. "Yes I can," she said. "Your powers are fading even more than before." Then Alita looked back to Kit. "I don't suppose you'd…" She gestured to her wet foot.

Kit smiled, focused her mind on Alita's dripping toes for a second and murmured, "*Sec!*"

"Thanks!" said Alita, waggling her now-dry toes before putting her sock and shoe back on.

"Are you all here just to go paddling, or do you have something to say?" asked Morag grumpily.

"Your powers are fading, as you can see," said Kit. "But we can help you get them back."

At that, the mermaids burst out laughing. "You?" Morag gestured to Faith. "Her, I'd believe, maybe. But you're a barely trained child wizard!"

"Actually, it was Alita and Josh who came up with the answer," said Kit.

"And we're not wizards at all," said Alita.

"We're very well trained though," said Josh. "Alita's got to grade five on the piano and I can say hello in nine languages. *Bonjour! Nnọọ! Halló! Sal—*"

"So spit it out. What is this wonderful magical solution you're offering us?" interrupted Morag.

Alita explained. "You draw your wild magic from Lizzie, just as wizards draw theirs from dragons, and saltfolk draw theirs from krakens."

Morag looked a little hesitant. "We do?" Then she shook her head. She appeared to be listening to something. "Doesn't matter! This loch is ours! Merfolk only!"

"Merfolk for merfolk!" chorused the other mermaids. Their eyes seemed glazed over, Kit thought.

"But if you want to keep yourselves to yourselves, you need your powers," said Alita. "If you allow Lizzie to return to the loch, your powers will return. And you'll be able to hide yourselves from prying human eyes again. And no one will be able to dip their toes in your loch." Alita waved her foot to reinforce her point.

"Of course, you don't *have* to let Lizzie return," said Kit. "We could leave you alone now, and keep Lizzie with us … and you could grow weaker and weaker until every day ends up being a human pool party in the loch. I bet you'd like to share your loch with a giant inflatable, wouldn't you? And lots of screaming toddlers in armbands?"

"And you'll probably get found by scientists coming for a swim and end up in a zoo," said

Josh. Then he thought about this. "Well, it would probably be an aquarium, not a zoo."

"I don't think you need to be quite so accurate in your threats, Josh," said Faith, trying not to smile.

Morag said nothing. She just narrowed her round eyes.

Kit glanced at the others. "Perhaps we're

wasting our time here? Let's leave these mermaids alone. Well, not alone for *long*."

"Wait!" said Morag. "Don't be hasty." She held up a webbed hand. "Wait. Let me talk to my people."

Kit nodded, and folded her arms, as if she was impatient to leave. "I'll give you a minute. Then we're going."

The mermaids clustered together, in a circle. Their voices were too low to catch, so Kit put a finger to her lips and whispered, "*Broadcast the quiet, ymhelaethu!*"

"… we have to let the Lesser Nessie back," Morag was saying. "Better to have Lizzie in our lake than a gaggle of humans!"

"Agreed," said one of the others. "I don't want to end up in the aquarium! They might put us in the same tank as a shark! Or, worse, a really annoying octopus!"

"That's settled then," said Morag. "We bring Lizzie back."

She turned to Kit and began to swim forward. She opened her mouth to speak. But then another voice rang out instead. A high, strange voice, which sounded as if it came from far away.

"*Don't give in, Morag,*" it said. "*If you do as we say, we will give you power again. A power more ancient than human wizardry. We will protect your loch. Don't give in just yet…*"

Morag's face froze. She looked as though she was suddenly very far away. She hesitated.

Kit didn't like the look of this. "Well, what's your answer?" she said.

Morag didn't reply. She was waiting for something. For the voice to speak again?

"Do not waver. This loch is yours. Don't let that beast return. We will protect you from outsiders. This loch is for merfolk only, remember that. When we return, you will have more power than ever. Trust us…"

Kit looked at her friends. They were just staring at Morag, looking confused.

"Are you hearing this?" she asked them. She looked at Faith.

"No, I can't hear anything," said Faith. Her forehead gathered into a frown of concentration.

"What can you hear?"

"A voice. Or maybe lots of voices. They sound … familiar. They're saying something about giving the mermaids power … protecting them from outsiders," Kit said. She blinked, trying to recall what the voice had said. But it was already fading from her mind.

Faith spoke a spell that Kit didn't recognise, then listened. "Still nothing," she sighed. "Somehow it's a voice that only Kit can hear."

"Me and the mermaids," said Kit. She pointed at Morag, who was staring into space. "She's waiting for it to speak again."

"Hmm," said Faith thoughtfully. "That's odd."

The voice – or many voices – appeared again in Kit's head. This time, the voice felt closer, as though it was coming from deep inside her brain. It was as loud and jolting as an alarm clock.

"Only the child can defeat us. Send her away."

Kit blinked for a moment. What WAS that voice?

"The answer is no," said Morag, turning to Faith and the children. Her face had a faraway look and her voice sounded almost robotic. "Go away. We can look after our own. Merfolk for merfolk!" she cried, slapping her scaly chest with her webbed palm.

"Merfolk for merfolk!" the others chimed in.

And they dived under the water, tails flapping in the air, and were gone.

"The voices you heard ... what were they like?" asked Faith, as the water became still again.

Kit shivered. "Something... I can't describe them. They were very high and very far away. It was as though they were inside my mind. They felt…" She shook her head. There were no words for what hearing that voice felt like. She just knew she never wanted to hear it again.

"They said I was the only one who could defeat them," she said.

At that, Faith looked worried. "I see," she said.

"I don't like the sound of that," said Josh. "If a gang of evil wizards thinks Kit is the only one who can defeat them … well. In books, evil wizards who are afraid of children try to kill those children. Or, at the very least, imprison them forever in a dungeon made of burning glass, like Malvolio did in book one of Danny Fandango."

Kit gulped. She didn't like the sound of either option.

"We don't know they're evil wizards. The voices, I mean," Duncan pointed out. "We just know that they're controlling the mermaids. Making them keep Lizzie away. For some reason…" His dark eyebrows knit together, thoughtful.

"How do we find out who they are?" asked Kit.

"How do we STOP them controlling the mermaids? And get them out of my head? It's *my* head; I don't like having other people talking in it! Especially not spooky voices that are out to get me!"

Duncan stroked his beard. "I have an idea. Let's go and see a friend of mine. She lives round the corner. She might have a few ideas about who's behind this."

"Who's your friend?" asked Kit.

"You'll see," said Duncan. He beckoned them all to follow him.

"Where's he taking us?" Kit asked Faith as they trooped outside and into the mobile library van.

"No spoilers," said Faith with a grin.

Duncan drove them through the hills, along winding little bumpy roads. Kit thought it was a shame to be stuck in the back of the van, without a view. But when they stopped and got out of the mobile library, she gasped. She was standing in the midst of a towering forest of white poles. A WHOMP

WHOMP WHOMP noise filled the air.

"It's a wind farm," said Duncan. "It's how we get our power out here, apart from the solar panels." He looked up at the sun, which was high in the midday sky, but half covered with clouds. "We don't get a LOT of sun," he admitted.

Near the base of one of the gigantic wind turbines, where the van was parked, was a little post with a plug in it. Duncan pulled a cord out of a flap in the back of his van and plugged it in.

"Now, we can leave that charging while we go and pay my friend a visit."

Kit looked around. There were no buildings, and definitely no people, anywhere nearby.

"Are we going to walk?" asked Josh in a worried voice. He looked down at his pristine-white trainers, then at the mossy, muddy ground, with the expression of someone being asked to throw a puppy into a shark tank.

"Walk where?" said Duncan. "We're already here." He opened his palm and held it up to the sky.

"*Foss gell cheh nah hed be owl.*"

The earth where they stood began to sink, ever so slowly.

Kit felt Josh grip her arm. "Whoa! Earthquake!" he said. "No, wait. Spell. Don't panic."

"I wasn't panicking," said Kit. "And you're hurting my arm."

"Sorry," said Josh as he let go.

They sank into the ground. At first they seemed to be travelling down a shaft with earthen walls but soon the walls began to fade, and they found themselves in a vast space.

The little tuft of grass they stood on was floating down through the air like a grassy magic carpet. Below them came a faint glow of green. A familiar glow.

Kit peeked over the edge of the tuft of moss that was carrying them down and down and down. The green glow grew stronger.

"It's a book wood!" she gasped.

"It's even bigger than the one at our library!" said Josh.

"It's the only wizard library for miles around," said Duncan. "So it can expand as far as it likes."

Alita was staring in silent awe. Finally, as their tuft of moss touched down lightly on the ground of the Book Wood, she said, with a voice trembling in excitement, "Duncan, does this mean we're going to meet your dragon?"

CHAPTER 10

SHADOWS
AROUND
A FLAME

The dragon's cave was much like Draca's lair,
although it was much bigger. The dragon was
bigger too. The hum of its magic was not the
familiar warmth of Draca's power, but something
colder. Something … older, Kit thought, though she
wasn't sure how she knew this.

The dragon's scales were red, whereas Draca's
were green. Its face was broader and its snout was
shorter. Its wings were vast, spread out on either
side of its body like the wings of a plane.

"Shall we go and say hello?" asked Duncan.

He didn't have to ask twice.

The children were already by the dragon's side,

holding hands with Kit and Faith. Kit looked to Faith, who looked to Duncan, and he nodded. Kit put her hand on the dragon. So did Faith. So did Duncan. Then everything went black.

In the dragon's dream, the cave became a beach.

The dragon was spread on a giant sunlounger, wearing sunglasses and drinking a fruity drink with pineapple bits in it. A whale leaped out of the bright-blue ocean and crashed back down, splashing them all.

"Ah," said Duncan. "I've been reading her a lot of travel books lately. She's clearly been enjoying them. This is Nath," he added, gesturing to the dragon.

The dragon, Nath, was watching them curiously over her sunglasses. "Humans," she said. "Humans who aren't Duncan. That's unusual."

She lay back on the sunlounger for a moment, letting out a sigh that blossomed from between her lips in a slow cloud of flame. "Humans are so new. I remember the time before. Now THAT was something."

"The time before humans?" asked Alita.

"Oh, so long before humans," said Nath. "A time when magic was everywhere, in the open, unafraid. A time before the masters came and made us fall asleep."

"The Dragon Masters," murmured Faith. "The ones who killed the dinosaurs. Ancient wizards. Ancient, *evil* wizards. As the stories go, they're the ones who made the dragons sleep, to harness their power. And once, they killed a dragon, hoping to absorb its power. It didn't work out so well for them – or for the dinosaurs."

"But wait…" Josh was frowning so deeply Kit though he might fold his entire forehead in two. "How can evil wizards have killed the dragon that killed the dinosaurs?" asked Josh. He threw up his hands in disbelief. "Surely you know that the dinosaurs died out millions of years before humans arrived? There can't have been wizards then!"

"Did I say they were *human* wizards?" asked Faith.

Josh's eyes widened. "WOW. If they weren't human, what were they?"

"Nobody knows," said Faith.

Kit felt that was enough about ancient wizard history.

"We were wondering if you could help us," she said to Nath. "We're here to help Lizzie come home. Some mermaids are being controlled by a spell, and they've chased Lizzie away. Do you know who's controlling them?"

At the edges of the beach, shadows began to gather. A storm filled the sky, and Nath seemed to shrink. There was a skitter of movement out of the corner of Kit's eye. She shuffled closer to her friends. "I have been having dark dreams," said Nath. "Of dead things. Of ancient things. Of bones. Of rats."

At that moment, a rat scuttled over Kit's feet. She yelled at the top of her lungs.

"Sorry," said Nath. "I was thinking of the rats again and … they appeared. When I think of a thing, I make it real. For you are in my mind. In my dream."

Faith, Duncan and the children came closer to the dragon.

"Do the rats you're seeing have anything to do with who's controlling the mermaids?" asked Faith.

That reminded Kit of something, at the edges of her brain. Blue eyes. Skeletal cheeks. But she couldn't grasp the image and it melted.

The dragon took a deep breath and blew out smoke rings before she answered.

"I can't see them clearly. The spellmakers. They're on the edges of my vision. They're long ago and far away. They're dancing like shadows round a flame." Nath looked at Kit. "And you're the flame."

She threw back her head and let out a terrifying roar. "Go away! You're bringing trouble! GO AWAY!"

Kit started to back away.

"Nath! Why are you being like this?" asked Duncan. He turned to Kit. "Sorry, she's usually so gentle … but I think we should go."

"Goodbye, Nath," said Faith.

The world went black.

CHAPTER 11

THE POWER OF THREE

"I don't think your dragon likes me very much," said Kit, when they got back to Duncan's house.

"Don't mind her," said Duncan. "She's just scared. I'm sorry she wasn't more helpful. Dragons can be vague at the best of times, but something's really got her spooked."

"What did she mean about me being a flame?" asked Kit. She pictured the lasers coming out of her eyes and shuddered.

"Nath doesn't always speak in ways that humans can follow," said Duncan. "She's very old and has slept a long time. But I think she meant that whoever or whatever is doing this is drawn to you.

Like a moth is drawn to a flame."

Kit realised that Faith was looking at her intently. "What do you think it means, Kit? Dig deep."

Kit tried to focus. She thought about the voice, and how it sounded. She thought about the lake. Then, for an instant, her mind cleared. The dream she'd forgotten bubbled up to the surface of her brain.

"Rats," she murmured. "I think that's what I dreamed of, when I fell asleep after we had our apple pie."

"At second breakfast, you mean," corrected Josh.

"You dreamed of rats?" asked Alita, giving Josh a look.

"I think it was a rat's skull," said Kit, trying to picture the details of her dream. "With glowing blue eyes. Then this skeleton jumped out of the water at me, and I woke up. What does it mean?" she asked.

Faith shrugged her shoulders. "That's the trouble

with dreams. They're not like books. They never come with footnotes to explain their meanings. Sometimes they don't mean anything. But when a dragon and a wizard have the same dream…" She trailed off, looking thoughtful. "That's not a coincidence."

"It could be a prophecy," piped up Josh. "Maybe Kit is seeing the future in her sleep?"

"So my future involves dead rats? Nice," said Kit.

"Prophecies aren't as straightforward as that," said Faith. "But hopefully Kit hasn't developed a talent for prophecy. That would make life too predictable. Who wants to know what's coming? Isn't half the fun of life finding out?"

"I don't like surprises," said Josh. "They make me jump."

A moment later he pointed at the leather-bound book on his lap, which was so big he had to stretch to turn the pages. "I've found something."

From where Kit was sitting, she could feel a

hum of magic buzzing through the book on Josh's lap.

"I've found a spell that breaks mind-control spells, and it says you don't need to know who's done the spell, just who it's been done TO." He looked up in triumph.

Faith took the book from Josh. "Good eye, Josh. This should do perfectly."

Josh beamed.

"Ah, it's a three spell," said Faith.

"Three what?" asked Alita.

Josh put his hand up. "Oh, I know!"

Faith raised an eyebrow. "We're not in school, Josh."

Josh lowered his hand. "Sorry," he said. "The spell needs three wizards to perform it."

"Right. Good thing we're all here then. We three can perform the spell," said Faith, gesturing at Duncan and Kit.

Kit's heart soared.

"We'll keep an eye on you in case of any more

… explosions," said Faith. "Duncan and I can help you stay in control and keep you steady."

Kit's heart de-soared.

"And I can help with the hand gestures if you can't remember the order of them," said Josh.

"What shall I do?" asked Alita eagerly.

"You could take Dogon for a walk?" Kit suggested. "Keep him away from where we're doing the spell so he doesn't distract us."

Alita's face fell. "Oh," she said in a small voice. "That's fine. I'll take Dogon. I'll go now and meet you all back here."

"Wait, Alita," said Kit, sensing that she'd done something wrong but not sure what it was.

"Bye!" said Alita. "Come, Dogon!" she said, then whistled. Dogon fluttered towards her.

"Come on," said Faith. "Let's go and free some mermaid minds."

They arrived near the lake and made sure to stop where they were not so close that the mermaids would spot them, but close enough for the magic to take hold. Duncan handed the book to Josh, open at the right page.

"Right, now we have our hands free to gesture," said Faith. "Thanks, Josh."

"Happy … to … help…" said Josh, gritting his teeth. "This book ... is … quite … heavy."

"We'll say the spell quickly then!" said Kit.

They began the spell. The words were simple and the gestures were all ones Kit had used before. With a spellbook this powerful, no fancy gestures or complicated phrases were needed. Josh mouthed the words alongside her all the same, which she found half annoying, half comforting.

"*Liberay hugur, break…*" she chanted, with Faith and Duncan.

As they spoke, Kit felt a power building inside her. Was it the spell taking hold? Was it working? The hum of magic grew stronger and stronger… until, with a bright green flash and a deafening BANG!

she felt a flood
of magic rush
through her
body, from
her toes
through
her chest
to the top
of her head,
and she was
blown through
the air, falling
heavily on to her
hands and knees.

Out of the corner of her eyes, Kit thought she saw movement. Something skittering away into the heather. She saw the flash of a pink tail. Then another. And another.

Then, while she knelt dazed on the ground, she heard three voices begin to chant again. Duncan, Faith and … Josh.

"Liberay hugur, break ... glee matsy angina. Liberay!"

Kit looked up at the others, blinking in surprise. "Josh?"

Duncan offered her a hand, but she scrambled to her feet on her own.

"What happened?" she asked, still feeling dazed.

"Your power burst out midway through. A more extreme version of what happened earlier. Josh finished the spell for you."

Josh beamed. "Well, everyone knows that you never leave a spell half finished!" he said. "And since Kit fell over, I thought I should try. Even though I'm not a wizard, so it was a bit dangerous." He looked a little pale, like he was only just realising what he'd done.

Duncan slapped him on the back. "Good lad. You made the right call."

Kit glanced down at her hands. They looked normal. But she felt very drained. She wobbled slightly on her feet. "What's wrong with me?" she whispered. "Am I … broken?" asked Kit.

"No, of course not," said Faith. She put a hand on Kit's shoulder. "I'm sorry, I shouldn't have asked you to do the spell while you were like this."

Kit felt like crying. She wanted to ask, *what if I'm always like this? What if I can never do spells again?*

Duncan came over to her. "You look a bit green," he said. "Are you OK?"

"I think so," said Kit.

"Would you like to go and lie down on my sofa?" offered Duncan.

"Maybe you should eat a biscuit?" suggested Josh. "That helped last time you went a bit…" He gestured an explosion around his head. "Boom!"

Kit shook her head. *I ruined the spell*, she thought. *My magic is out of control. I can't be trusted. Josh had to risk himself because I failed.* "I'm fine," she said. "I might go and see if I can find Alita. Will you be here still?"

"Yup," said Faith. "Don't worry. You go and clear your head."

Kit looked down at her hands again, biting her lip a little. Tears were pricking at the edges of her eyes.

She rushed off before the pricking tears risked coming out of her eyes in a flood. She walked quickly over the purple heather, breathing in the wet smell of the land. However fast she walked, her mind whirred faster. *What if my magic's broken? What if I'm dangerous? What if Lizzie can never come home, and Dogon will have to stay here, and it's all my fault?*

Mid-thought, she saw a shape in the sky just over the hill. She broke into a run and, getting closer, saw that it was Dogon. Alita was sitting on a stone watching the creature, with a distant look on her face.

"Alita!" Kit called.

Alita turned and waved. Dogon fluttered down on to her shoulder.

"Have you finished the spell?" asked Alita, as Kit drew closer. "Are the mermaids back to normal?"

Kit shook her head. "My magic went wrong again and messed everything up," she said. "Josh finished the spell to stop things getting worse."

"Josh is clever like that," said Alita. She didn't sound entirely pleased about it. Kit took a seat on the cool stone next to her friend. They both watched Dogon for a moment. Then Alita spoke up.

"It's going to be OK, you know. I'm sure Faith will work out what's up with your magic."

"But what if she can't? What if it's permanent?" The thought was terrible.

"Well, even if your magic is going wrong, at least you HAVE magic," said Alita in a quiet voice.

Kit turned to her friend and noticed for the first time that her eyes were all red and puffy. She'd been crying. "Oh, Alita, are you OK?"

Alita shrugged and tried to smile. "I just feel … like there's nothing I can do to help Dogon. What if he can never go home? And Lizzie. What if she's stuck in England forever? I want to help, but I don't have your magic, I don't have Josh's brains. And…" She was starting to cry again. "I just feel like I'm in the way!"

"You're not in the way!" said Kit, almost angry

with Alita for thinking that. "You're my best friend!"

"But I can't do anything special," said Alita. Her mouth went small and tight, and Kit worried she might start crying again.

"Well, do you think I want to be friends with people because they have special powers or genius brains?" she asked. "Are you friends with *me* because I have magic powers?"

Alita frowned. "Well, no. We're friends because I like you." She picked up one of her plaits and started playing with it. "I feel like you're tricking me into feeling better."

"Is it working?" asked Kit.

"I think it is," said Alita. She broke out into a grin. "Kit Spencer, your magic powers may not be working right now, but your cheering-up powers are on fire."

Kit smiled. She realised that cheering up Alita was making herself feel better. That was a kind of magic too.

A shadow passed over her friend's face again.

"I'm still worried," said Alita. "I want to make it all OK again!"

"Me too," said Kit. "But at least Dogon doesn't seem worried!"

"No, he looks like he's having a brilliant time," agreed Alita. "I think he likes it out here."

Above them, Dogon was doing loop-the-loops, cruising on his back on the air currents at the top of each loop. As he cruised, he put his little paws behind his head like someone floating in the sea.

They watched Dogon for a moment, until he swooped down to land and trotted off over the hill.

"Dogon, where are you going?" called Alita.

The girls got up from the stone and followed him. When they caught up, he was digging in the heather. Then he put his little snout down and snapped something up with a chirrup and a chomping sound.

"What have you got there?" Alita asked. She reached her hand out, and Dogon backed away with a naughty look in his eye. "Oh, you want me to chase you, do you?"

Dogon kept backing away with a playful growl. Just as Alita started to run towards him to start the game of chase, Dogon let out a horrible whining sound, curling up into a sad little furry ball.

"Dogon!" cried Alita, running to him and kneeling down, taking the creature's head in her arms. "I think he's got something stuck in his throat," she said. She put her fingers into Dogon's mouth, fishing out a bone. As soon as it was free, Dogon gave a little snort, puffing out smoke and uncurling himself. Then he started to lick Alita's hand gratefully, nuzzling close to her.

Kit leaned down to stroke Dogon, when Alita gave a hiss. "OUCH!" She hurriedly dropped the bone that she'd been holding. On her palm was a strange mark, like a little curly x. "Oh," said Alita. "It doesn't hurt any more but … that's odd."

Kit peered at the mark. "I think that's

magical," she said. "That's not just a burn mark or something. It's too ... curly."

She knelt down to look at the bone. It looked perfectly ordinary, like something you'd see left over after you'd eaten roast chicken for Sunday lunch.

Alita knelt beside her. "I think that's from a mammal. It might be an upper leg bone."

"You know weird stuff," said Kit approvingly. "Now, we need to take this back to Faith to look at."

"I don't know," said Alita. "Maybe we shouldn't get close to it, after…" She held up her palm. The x was starting to fade, but Kit could still see its faint outline.

"Can you do a spell to lift it?" suggested Alita.

"But … my magic might still be going crazy. What if it goes wrong and I shoot flames out of my eyeballs again and I hurt you?"

"It's fine." Alita shrugged. "I'll stand well back. If anyone gets their eyebrows singed, it'll be you." She smiled.

Kit swallowed, and prepared herself for a simple lifting spell.

"*Levantar!*" she said, gesturing at the bone to lift in the air. It wobbled for a moment, then slowly raised itself into the air. There was no green flash, no bang, and nothing went wrong. Kit kept her arm raised, holding the bone out in front of her, hovering in the air, just to be safe. Dogon kept well back, sitting on Alita's shoulder.

"You did it!" said Alita.

"Now, I just need to keep focusing on it until we get back to the others…"

They walked quietly towards the lake.

When Faith saw them coming, with the floating object in front of them, she did a double take. "What … is that?" she asked, breaking into a jog, her braids swaying and her jewellery jangling.

"Don't touch it!" warned Kit.

"Noted!" said Faith. She spoke a spell of her own, pulling the object through the air towards her with a swiping gesture.

Duncan came to look at it. "Looks like rat bone. Although it's about ten times too big."

Josh came over to join Kit and Alita while Faith and Duncan inspected the bone, which was hovering between them now.

"What did we miss here?" asked Kit.

"Not much," said Josh. "They've just been trying a few spells to work out what went wrong, but nothing yet. Where did you find the bone?"

"We didn't," said Alita. "Dogon did." Dogon

was a little way off, rolling around in the heather.

"What's that on your hand?" Josh asked.

Alita showed him her fading cross.

Josh gasped. "Alita, I know that mark! I've read about it in one of the books in the Stacks. You need to show it to Faith NOW."

"Why?" asked Alita, massaging her palm, her eyes suddenly wide with fear.

"Because that's the mark left by a spell," said Josh. "That bone is cursed."

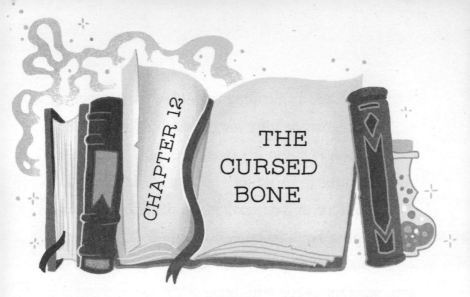

CHAPTER 12

THE CURSED BONE

There was a lot of fuss after that. Duncan and Faith did a cleansing spell on Alita and Dogon on the spot. "That should tide you over until we can get you home," said Duncan. They were striding across the heather towards his home underground. "I have some herbs there that I can use to wipe away the effects of the curse on anyone who's touched it."

When they got back, Faith busied herself creating a safe place to put the bone and Duncan created a healing potion.

After a few minutes, he returned with two stinking eggcups full of a browny-green goop, handing one to each of the girls.

"I didn't touch the bone! I feel fine," objected Kit.

"You were near it for longer than the rest of us though. Best to be on the safe side," said Duncan. He made her take the eggcup.

"I don't have to be on the safe side, do I?" asked Josh, edging away from them on the sofa. "I like the dangerous side, where I don't have to drink that."

"You should be fine," laughed Duncan.

"Good," said Josh. "Because it smells worse than the sewage treatment plant behind my uncle's house. It smells like something that's been living at the back of the fridge for a year, boiled in sick."

"Can you stop describing it?" begged Alita.

"Yeah, we're the ones who actually have to drink it!" growled Kit.

"Sorry," said Josh, looking more relieved than sorry.

Kit peered into her eggcup and gave a sniff. Josh was right. It was foul. She immediately regretted ever growing a nose.

"It might smell horrible," said Duncan. "But,

believe me, drinking this is a thousand times better than whatever might happen when a curse kicks in…"

Kit and Alita exchanged glances. "Same time?" suggested Kit.

Alita nodded. "Hold your nose!" she said.

They both did, and knocked back their potions.

"DISGUSTING!" choked Kit.

"Urrrrrr!" coughed Alita.

Dogon, meanwhile, was lapping hungrily at a saucer full of his potion.

"Why is Dogon's so tasty?" asked Kit.

"You can't persuade a pup that something's for their own good, so you have to make their potions tasty," said Duncan.

"Remind me to be less easy to persuade next time," said Kit.

"Let's hope there's NO next time," said Faith. She had crossed the room to join them on the squishy chairs and sofa. She was holding a glowing box that appeared to be made out of light. With a gesture, it rose into the air, rotating slowly. It was almost solid-looking, but Kit could just about make out a little white object at its heart. The bone.

"This will stop it doing any harm to any of us," said Faith, gesturing to the box. "It's sort of a magical trap. To stop the bone cursing anyone else."

"Phew!" said Josh.

"So we're definitely safe?" said Alita. She was looking down at her hand nervously. Dogon, who'd finished his potion, hopped up on to the sofa beside her and rested his furry muzzle in her lap.

"Completely," said Duncan. "Curse-free."

"So," said Faith. "Shall we run some tests on this bone?"

"What kind of tests?" asked Josh.

"I thought I'd try a backtrace spell, to see where the spell came from that cursed this bone. Perhaps it's the same group of wizards controlling the mermaids."

"What's a backtrace spell?" asked Kit.

"Oh, oh, I know this!" said Josh. He didn't put his hand up, but Kit could tell that he really wanted to.

Faith nodded to him. Her mouth was twitching towards a smile, but she kept serious. "Go on."

"It's like … you know on police TV shows, where the police are on the phone to a bad guy, and they try to keep the bad guy on the phone, so they can use computers to check where the bad guy's calling from. It's like that, but without police or computers and with magic. It's a spell to find out where a spell's coming from and going to," he finished.

"Definitely no computers or police," said Faith. "But that's it exactly. It uses scrying magic."

Scrying magic is for finding out information. I remember it by thinking about "prying". My grandma always says "Don't pry" when she wants me to mind my own business.

"Let me show you," Faith went on. "Duncan, do you have a map of the area?"

"Aye." He got up and went to rustle through some papers on a shelf.

Kit sat up eagerly, ready to learn a new spell.

She wasn't disappointed.

When Duncan laid a map down on the coffee table, Faith began.

"To the keld, connect!"

Faith gestured to the bone in its shining cage, then raised her hands out to the side, then directly to the sky, then to the ground. A hum began deep in the ground, rising up through Kit, through the room, through the earth. The bone began to spin in its cage, faster and faster, until a flash of red light shot out from it, like a laser beam. It hit the map but didn't burn it, highlighting a spot in the middle.

"The loch," said Josh. "It's coming from the loch." He frowned. "Are the wizards who cursed the bone in the loch? Like, in scuba gear or something?"

The light faded. Faith shook her head. "No, they're not. Because the curse isn't coming from the loch."

"But the light from the bone went to the loch. Doesn't that mean the wizard who cursed this bone is there?"

"No," said Faith. "Because if that was the case, the light would have begun on the map, and spread to the bone. This went the other way round."

Kit didn't know what any of this meant. "What?" she said.

"So … the curse isn't going from a wizard to the bone?" said Alita thoughtfully. "It's going from the bone to the loch?"

Kit felt the cogs turn in her brain. The thoughts fell into place with satisfying, silent clicks. "There aren't any evil wizards doing this," she said. "It's the bone itself. The bone is controlling the mermaids!"

CHAPTER 13

THE ANCIENT CURSE

"A bone spreading a curse," said Alita. "That's creepy! I wonder who cursed it?"

"And how do we break the curse?" asked Kit.

"Before we can get any answers, we need to know what kind of curse we're dealing with. We'll need supplies," said Faith.

"Like herbs and stuff?" asked Alita.

"Magic potions?" asked Josh.

"No!" said Faith. "Food. I'm starving! It's definitely past lunchtime, and I can't think on an empty stomach."

"Me too!" said Kit. She looked at her watch. It was two thirty! No wonder her stomach was almost eating itself. Apple pie, biscuits and disgusting anti-curse juice were *not* enough to fuel a growing wizard into the afternoon.

Duncan made some cheese sandwiches, with Cheddar from a local farm; thick, fresh butter; and bread that he'd baked himself. Faith made a drink called chocolate tea, which involved grating little balls of chocolate that looked like dinosaur eggs, together with fresh nutmeg and cinnamon, then melting it all together on the stove with thick, creamy condensed milk. It was so delicious, Kit let out little yelps as she drank it.

Then they set to work.

Faith used her thaumometer to measure the magic coming off the bone. Its gem glowed a bright yellow, vibrating slightly as Faith held it. She widened her eyes. "Strong," she breathed. "And it's definitely mind magic. A control curse."

As she passed the device back and forth in front of the floating bone, Faith frowned. She looked at the thaumometer and shook it a few times.

"What's wrong?" asked Kit.

"I'm measuring the magical decay. That is, how old the curse is. And it's older than it should be. I think there might be something wrong with my thaum."

"How old is it saying it is?" asked Kit.

"About … I don't know exactly, but more than … fifty million years."

"Someone made this curse fifty million years ago?" Kit's brain boggled at the idea.

"Well, not someone human," said Josh. "There weren't humans then."

Kit remembered something. She turned to Faith. "You said the Dragon Masters were wizards … but they weren't human." She pointed at the bone. "Could they have made this curse? Back before they killed the dinosaurs? And themselves?"

"Oh." Faith sat bolt upright. She got up and went over to the bone, peering into its glass case. "Kit, I think you're right." Her face was full of wonder. "We could be looking at one of the last spells the Dragon Masters cast before they died."

"This is a piece of wizard history," said Duncan. "It belongs in the Museum of Magic! Or it will do once we've broken the curse."

"Seriously," said Faith. "I know a curator who

will literally scream when I tell him about this."

"Dogon's a clever little historian for finding it," said Alita, giving the creature a few scratches behind his ears.

"I wonder what triggered the curse?" said Duncan. "The bone must have been here for a very long time. Why did it start affecting the mermaids now?"

"Maybe one of them found it in the loch?" suggested Alita. "Like Dogon did. And threw it out of the water without realising what it was?"

"But by then they'd all touched it and it was too late!" said Kit. She could just picture the grumpy mermaids throwing away the bone, slowly starting to fall under the thing's cursed spell.

Josh was pacing up and down, his giant brain clearly throbbing with ideas. "So the mermaids triggered the curse … and then the bone started to control them. Why did it make them chase Lizzie away?"

"And why did it say I'm the only one who

can stop it?" said Kit. "Why's it talking to the mermaids? Can curses talk?"

"Good question!" said Faith.

"I asked a good question?" asked Kit, surprised.

"Don't sound so surprised," said Faith.

"It can't just be a simple curse," said Duncan. "The bone seems to be … thinking."

This was all getting a bit much for Kit. "How can a bone think?"

Faith peered at the bone. "I believe – though I'm not sure – that the Dragon Masters bound a little bit of their essence to this bone. So when they died, their minds stayed behind. It's called a will curse. The most powerful of all curses. And, clearly, the longest-lasting."

"Millions of years long!" said Josh, impressed.

Kit blinked. This hurt her brain. "I still don't get why they're controlling the mermaids?"

"Neither do I," said Faith. "And I don't like not knowing."

"What can we do? We still have to break the

curse," said Alita. "Or the mermaids will keep Lizzie away, and Dogon will never be able to go home!"

"Not to mention what's probably happening back at home, the longer Lizzie stays there," muttered Faith.

Alita looked worried. "Will everyone back at home be OK?"

Faith waved off her worry. "Oh, it won't be dangerous. It will just be … awkward to explain to the Wizards' Council."

Alita nodded, relieved.

"What breaks curses like this?" asked Kit.

"Wild magic," said Faith. "Wildness breaks up the will of the curse caster and splits it apart from the cursed object."

"Oh! So can we use Nath's magic?" asked Kit.

Faith shook her head. "A dragon's magic would be too raw, too fierce. It would hurt the mermaids."

"We can use the wild magic of nature!" suggested Duncan. "In every blade of grass, there's a tiny trace of wild magic. And in every ant and every animal." He waved his hand at the round windows, looking out on the rolling heather.

"Hmm," said Faith, thinking. "We need to focus the wild magic in nature on the bone, and on the mermaids, to break the curse."

"This book says crystals are good for focusing magic," said Josh. "Do you have any?"

"Yes, but none big enough," said Duncan.

"I have a question," said Alita, who'd been silent for a while. "Do we have to do a spell to gather up all the wild magic? Can't we just gather creatures instead? And take them to the mermaids. Would that work?"

"Genius!" cried Faith. "That, Alita, is a stroke of genius!"

Kit thought Josh looked ever so slightly annoyed at that. But Alita's face lit up like a star. "Really?" she said.

"How do we get animals to gather though?" asked Josh. "Like, use a sheepdog?"

"Don't worry about that," said Duncan. "I have my ways. Alita, perhaps you and Kit could help me?"

"Excellent," said Faith. "Then Josh and I will find exactly the right spell to channel that wild nature magic and break the curse."

"So I don't have to go and chase after ants and stuff?" asked Josh.

"No chasing. Just reading," Faith replied.

"This *is* a genius plan!" Josh declared.

CHAPTER 14
MORE THAN TWO OF EVERY ANIMAL

Out in the heather, Duncan showed Kit how to do some spells to round up animals. But it wasn't as easy as he made it look. Kit's magic wasn't misfiring or anything – she wasn't feeling any of that intense build-up of energy, and there were no laser blasts coming out of her eyes. She just … couldn't get the animals to follow her.

"You have to be gentle, Kit," said Duncan. "With this type of magic, it's not about control, it's about love. You have to show the animals kindness. You have to help them come with you."

"I don't think I have a gentle mode," said Kit.

"Try," said Duncan.

Kit grumbled and tried again, speaking the spell Duncan had showed her. She bowed down towards the creatures, opening out her arms and saying the spell word, "*Com!*"

She waited.

"Be gentle," said Duncan.

"OK, animals. I love you all. Now, come here! *Com!*"

Meanwhile, Alita had already found a colony of beetles, and a pheasant, managing to tempt it on to her shoulder with some biscuit crumbs. Dogon fluttered around, making persuasive noises too. Kit wasn't sure if he was helping or getting in the way, but Alita was doing impressive work.

Kit only managed to persuade two rabbits and a worm to come with her in the end. And with the worm it was less about persuasion and more about picking it up and carrying it.

Duncan kept the creatures with them, weaving his spells around them with murmured words. He drew a herd of deer towards them. The majestic creatures walked slowly over the purple heather, eyes bright and eager, making a strange low noise in their throats that sounded like something from the beginning of time.

"They're lovely!" said Alita.

One of the deer, a large stag with many-branched antlers, came over to her and bent his head. Alita nervously petted his neck. He made a snuffling sound.

"I think he likes you," said Duncan. He was giving Alita a strange look. "You really do seem to have the knack of this."

Alita was giggling as the stag nuzzled her hand.

"This is literally her idea of heaven," said Kit.

"Well. Heaven can wait," said Duncan. "We have work to do."

They met Josh and Faith down by the lake just before four o'clock. Josh's jaw dropped as they approached. Even Faith looked deeply impressed.

"Well, Noah, you've got more than two of every animal there," she said to Duncan.

"I only got about two in total," said Kit. "Alita got loads!"

"Did she? Well done, Alita!" said Faith. She gave Alita an odd look, then glanced over to Duncan, who raised an eyebrow.

Alita looked puzzled. "What was that about?" she whispered to Kit.

"Dunno," said Kit. "Grown-ups always like having their secret languages."

A crowd of animals walked behind them. There were pheasants and deer, rabbits and grouse, as well as seabirds, summoned from the sea, and eagles and ospreys. Bees buzzed and butterflies flapped their multicoloured wings. The ground crawled with insects, from beetles and ants to weevils and snails. (The snails brought up the rear.) Field mice and voles scuttled around them, and Highland cattle, Shetland ponies and sheep tramped behind.

Duncan called a halt to his army of beasts with a gesture and a word. Dogon landed at the front of the army, puffing out his chest.

"Now," said Faith, "the bone…" She made a scooping gesture with her hand and the bone rose up in its glowing magical case.

"Shall we begin? Josh found the curse-breaking spell," said Faith. "It needs three wizards." Faith looked at Kit, her black eyes shining. "What do you say, Kit?"

"But … I'm not safe," said Kit. "We still don't know what's making my magic flare up. Shouldn't Josh do it? If it's a written spell, he can do it, can't he?"

Josh shook his head. "Not this one. It specifically needs wizards. Or the non-wizard person reading it explodes. And I don't want to explode."

"But what if my *magic* explodes and I hurt you all?" said Kit.

"I believe in you," said Faith. "All you need to

do is say the spell … and use as little of your power as you can. Almost try NOT to do magic. Just let the magic of nature do the work. Does that make sense?"

"I … think so," said Kit. Her heart was beating fast, like a speaker, thumping a bassline in her chest.

"Let's begin," called Duncan. "The animals are starting to grow restless." Just then a pheasant squawked loudly, and a deer let out a throaty bellow.

The surface of the lake beyond them began to ripple, and the mermaids rose up.

"What's all that noise?" shrieked Morag. "Didn't we tell you to leave? Come closer and I'll bite you. We'll scratch out your eyes. LEAVE US, MORTALS!"

Faith ignored them as they carried on yelling threats and promises of bites. "Take my hand," she said to Duncan.

Duncan took the hand she offered and nodded,

showing that he was ready.

He beckoned the animals closer. Alita helped to herd them in the right direction, whispering to them.

Kit glanced at Faith. Faith nodded and reached out her hand to Kit. Kit took it, as Faith whispered, "Don't be afraid. You have the power. You are safe. You can do this."

Kit wasn't sure. Was she making a horrible mistake?

Tingling power ran through her. Not Faith's power. Her own power. She could feel it trying to burst out from her. But she pushed it down, thinking of her friends, of keeping them safe. *Just say the words*, she told herself. *Try NOT to do magic.*

They began to speak the spell.

A hum filled the air. The animals behind them shifted and rumbled. Alita stood beside them and stroked the face of the stag, whispering calming words.

Kit spoke the words along with Duncan and Faith. She gripped their hands, as though holding on to a cliff edge with her fingertips. She pushed the magic inside her down and down to stop it bubbling up.

Still, Kit felt that dreadful power rising. The more she spoke, the stronger the feeling became.

She heard a voice. It was coming from the bone. *"The child can't defeat us. She's holding back."* Kit heard echoing, high-pitched laughter.

The magic grew within her. The soft magic of nature flowed through the animals, through the earth, through the plants, through the air itself.

Was she holding back? Would the words be enough, if she squashed down her magic?

That voice was laughing again.

"We will win. We are winning! This spell has failed!"

I can't let them win! she thought. Kit let a little of the magic rise in her. She felt it building, until her whole body felt as though it was on fire.

"Kit, what's wrong?" Josh's voice sounded very far away.

From among the animals came the pitter-pattering of dozens of little feet. No, hundreds. Kit saw rats running from the army of animals towards the loch.

So. Many. Rats.

"She's losing control!" said Faith. She, too, sounded very far away. Everything in Kit was going into the spell. She couldn't let that voice defeat her. She wouldn't let the Dragon Masters win.

"Kit. Control your power," said Faith. "Don't let it burst out. Control your power. It's your power, not theirs."

"*Let go*," said the voice. "*Let it all go. Or you won't defeat us.*"

Duncan and Faith began to speak the spell again. Kit joined in. She felt wave after wave of magic wash through her.

"The rats!" someone cried. "They're … joining."

Kit looked at the loch. On the water, the rats were climbing and clambering over one another. Floating on the water. Forming into another creature, made out of hundreds of rats. A giant monster, seething, rising. A rat the size of a bear. Kit wanted to scream.

"*So close*," said

the voice. "*Unleash your power. Free us.*"

Kit felt as though the magic in her was about to explode. She felt it would be so easy to just let go. To do what the voice wanted. "I don't think I can do this," she whispered.

Just then, she felt a tap on her shoulder. She paused and turned. Alita was there, with Dogon. She placed Dogon on Kit's shoulder and whispered, "Think of Dogon. Do this for all of us. Don't give up. Don't let go."

Someone gave her arm a squeeze. Josh was standing there. "You've got this, Kit," he said.

The rat beast swayed across the water towards them.

"*Give up,*" said the voice. The voice of the rats, speaking as one. "*Give us our true shape. Release all your power into us. Bring us back to life. We are so close...*"

NO, thought Kit. *My friends believe in me. I believe in me. So I refuse to be bossed around by ghost rat wizards from the dawn of time. I'm Kit*

Spencer, and I am not afraid of you.

In that moment, she realised something. Several somethings.

They lured me here, to Scotland. The Dragon Masters lured me here. They made the mermaids chase Lizzie away, knowing it would mess with my magic, knowing I'd follow the trail here. They need me here to bring them back. They've been taunting me, to get me to do what they want. They let me overhear them talking to the mermaids, about me being the only person who can beat them.

Well. They're right about that.

"ENOUGH!" she yelled.

"Kit?" whispered Faith, her face full of worry and pain. "Kit?"

"I'm OK," said Kit. "Let's finish this."

Faith nodded.

With that, Kit closed her eyes, pressed the rising magic down into the pit of her stomach, and spoke the last words of the spell in time with Duncan and Faith.

"BREAK!"

The mermaids were shrieking with rage. A rage that sounded like it was from another world, another time. An ancient rage.

Another voice shrieked even louder. The voice of the Dragon Masters. The ghost wizards. The cursers of the bone. The controllers of the mermaids.

A shock wave whooshed across the loch. The rats scattered, falling apart and splashing into the water, swimming away, each alone. The scream of the Dragon Masters cut through the air and then, suddenly, fell silent.

The mermaids let out a very different cry.

A whoop, almost. The glassy look in their eyes departed and they surged forward, swimming joyfully.

"FREEEEEEE!" shrieked Morag. "We're FREE!!"

"Freeeeee!" echoed the other merfolk.

The sky grew lighter. Sun broke through the clouds.

Kit saw dozens of rats swimming in different directions across the loch, making for dry land. There was no longer a single mind controlling them. They just wanted to get to safety.

"You DID it!" said Faith.

"It worked!" cried Kit. "I didn't lose control!" She threw her arms round Faith in a hug of joy. Alita hugged them both too, and Josh.

Duncan gestured to the animals. "Thank you!" he called.

With a whinny and a snuffle and a squawk and a peal of squeaks, they scattered, back to their lives.

"Is it over?" asked Josh.

"I think so," said Kit. "I think it is."

"What happened back there?" Faith asked Kit. "The rats … what were they?"

"I think … I think that was the Dragon Masters," said Kit. "They were trying to use my power to come back from the dead. They wanted me to lose control of my wild magic. I think that's what would have set them free."

"That must have been why they left the curse," said Josh, "sort of an escape hatch, when they died. A way for them to come back one day, when someone disturbed their bones."

"I hope they didn't leave too many other cursed bones around…" said Kit.

"Oh. You can bet that they did," said Faith grimly. "But we're safe for now."

"Er … I'm not a hundred per cent sure about that," said Alita. She was pointing back at the lake.

Dark clouds were forming above the lake. Thunder rumbled in the distance. Then a huge fork of lighting slashed down, sizzling into the lake. Smoke rose up from the surface of the water. Thick, swirling green smoke. Shapes formed in it. Kit thought that the shapes looked a little like skulls. The smoke writhed in and out of focus.

"What IS that?" yelled Alita above the din of the thunder.

"WE ARE HERE", said a voice. Kit thought she saw a shape in the mist. A rat-like face. Another. A claw. A hint of a swishing tail.

"YOU BROKE OUR

CURSE BUT YOU CANNOT STOP US. WE WILL RETURN. WE WERE ALWAYS HERE. WE WILL FIND A WAY".

"Go AWAY!" yelled Kit. "You lost! I defeated you! Stop hanging around like a bad smell, you bunch of stinky evil ghost rats!"

There was a high-pitched, terrifying scream, and the storm broke, rain hammering down on them. The faces in the smoke rushed towards Kit and through her, throwing her to the ground. She felt a chill rush through her, a smell of fire and decay and a horrible, horrible cold. She let out a cry, then felt hands pulling her to her feet. She looked back over her shoulder. The faces were gone. The mermaids had ducked beneath the water. There was nothing but the rain.

CHAPTER 15

CHOCOLATE TEA

Fifteen minutes later, they were sitting in Duncan's living room drinking some more chocolate tea. Duncan and Faith did a drying spell on them, but they all still felt in need of warmth and comfort, and not just because the Scottish weather was on the cool side.

"Are you OK?" Josh asked Kit.

Kit shivered, remembering how it felt when the rats had passed through her. "It felt… I can't put it into words," said Kit.

"Perhaps it's best not to," said Faith. "Words are powerful." She gave Kit a pat on the shoulder and got up, striding over to where the bone lay in its carrying case.

She reached in and plucked the bone out.

Seeing the look of horror on the children's faces, she added, "It's perfectly safe now. We broke the curse. But, Duncan, you said this looks like a mammal's bone? A rat?"

Duncan's eyes went wide. "Of course. It's much too big to be a modern rat but … a giant rat. Now we're talking."

"So the Dragon Masters were evil giant rats from the dawn of time?" said Josh.

"Cool!" said Kit. Then, remembering the rats again, she shuddered.

Faith gave her an intent look. "You're safe now. And, I suspect…" She pulled something out of her pocket. It was her thaumometer. She pointed it at Kit, who flinched a little, afraid of what it might say.

The thaumometer glowed ever so slightly. Faith's face broke into a gigantic smile. "You're back to normal! I thought so!" she said.

"Really?"
asked Kit.
She felt a
wash of relief,
followed by
a little doubt.
"Why is it
still glowing
then?"

"Oh, your
wild-magic
levels are
always a little
higher than
the average

wizard," said Faith, pocketing the thaum again.
"You're a wild one, Kit Spencer. I think that's why
the Dragon Masters chose you."

"They … chose me?" asked Kit. "Chose me for
what?"

"They needed someone to release them back

into this world," said Faith. "Someone with a naturally high store of wild magic. They wanted to ride back from the dead on a wave of your power."

"So that's why they were egging me on to let go during the spell?" Kit said. "I knew it!"

""Yes," said Faith. "They wanted you to let go! They scurried into your mind and threw your power out of balance. I wonder how though?"

"My dream!" gasped Kit. "They came in through my dream! When I fell asleep at lunch and dreamed of rats."

"Well, that's creepy," said Josh.

"Should we be worried that they said they'd be back?" asked Alita. "Will they try to get into Kit's dreams again?"

"They don't have an anchor in the world any more," said Faith. "Now that we've broken the curse that linked them to the bone. But if they try to get back another way, we'll be ready for them."

"I can't believe they TOLD us they were coming back," said Josh. He made a disapproving clicking sound with his tongue. "Man, ancient evil giant rat ghosts need to watch more movies. Evil villains should never reveal their plans. It's what gets them caught in the end!"

"Well, there probably weren't many movies in ancient times," pointed out Alita. "So there's no way they could know that."

Kit couldn't help laughing. Although there was a shadow hanging over her, her friends were so silly and she couldn't feel too dark.

Faith put a hand on her shoulder and gave her a squeeze. "Well done, Kit. You beat them. You can go home soon. There's just one more thing to do."

Duncan drove them all back to the lochside and they piled out, Dogon on Alita's shoulder.

Faith nodded to Josh, and he began to sing. This time, it was a hymn. Something about ancient feet. Kit didn't know it.

As he sang, the lake rippled. The lochfolk rose slowly and cautiously out of the water.

"Yes?" said
Morag. Her pale
eyes peered out
from between
the curtains of
her long weed-
hair. She looked
bleary, as though
she'd only just
woken up from a long,
restless sleep. "What is it?" she snapped.

"We've come to ask if Lizzie can come home again," called Alita.

"And if you mind going to fetch her," added Josh. "Because I have to be home for dinner by six."

"Me too!" said Alita. "She's already texted me three times to tell me she's making fresh pakoras, which is her way of saying don't be late without actually saying it."

"And my mum will make me eat my dinner

cold if I'm late," added Josh. "She learned that in a parenting book," he added, making a face. "The one type of book I DON'T like."

Morag looked at them blankly. "What's that? Feeling a bit funny. Could you repeat that?"

"I need to go home for dinner," repeated Josh. "Because my mum—"

"No, fool child, I mean, the part about Lizzie coming home. Is Lizzie not here? Where's she gone?"

"You threw her out," said Kit.

"Don't you remember?" asked Alita. "You told her she wasn't welcome any more and you chased her away."

From the look on her face, Morag clearly did not remember. She looked at the humans like they were pulling her tail. "No, she was just here a minute ago…" Morag gave a nod to one of the other merfolk, and he dived down below the surface. A moment later he popped up again and gave Morag a shrug.

"Not here, ma'am!" he said.

Morag narrowed her eyes. "What's going on? I was just…" She tailed off. "I'm not sure what just happened. But it happened when a troop of meddling wizards turned up at my lochside so it's probably your fault."

"No. It's really not," said Faith. "But … you don't remember anything?"

"Last thing I remember was finding a wee bone at the bottom of the loch. Didn't like the look of it. Threw it out." She gestured beyond the water. "Then…" She waved her webbed hands. "Nothing."

"You were under a curse," said Duncan. "We broke the curse."

Morag stared at him. "You what?"

"You were under a curse. We broke it. Now you can get Lizzie back and get your magic back," said Duncan. "A thank-you might be nice?" he suggested.

"HA!" trilled Morag. "Not likely. Where did Lizzie go?"

"You chased her away through a water portal," said Faith. "You should tell her to come back."

"Hmph! I suppose we will," said Morag. "Not because you asked, mind. Only because we want our magic back, so we can stop landscuttlers coming and gawping at us like this," she said to the other merfolk. "Let's go and tell that pesky plesiosaur to come home."

And, with a flick of her tail, she disappeared beneath the water.

"I thought that breaking the curse would stop them from being so mean," said Josh, looking disappointed.

A moment later, another head broke the surface of the lake. It was Lizzie.

She was grinning. "I don't know how you did it, but thank you!" said Lizzie. "Home sweet home!" She flapped her flippers and waggled her tail. "I was starting to feel proper cramped in that little pond," she said. "So ... thank you. I hope I didn't make too much mess. By the time I left ... er ... some things were happening."

"Things?" asked Faith. She narrowed her eyes. "THINGS?"

"Yes. And stuff. BYE!" said Lizzie, diving quickly under the water and swimming around, leaving a streak of ripples on the surface.

CHAPTER 16

HOME

They said goodbye to Duncan by the loch. He gave them each a paper bag full of homemade biscuits before they left. When he came to Alita he said, "That was good work with the animals. You're a natural."

"I was thinking of being a magical vet when I grow up," said Alita, smiling shyly. "If I don't decide to be a dragon-tamer. And if my parents don't mind."

"I'm sure we can find a way to persuade them," said Duncan, scratching behind Dogon's ears. Dogon gave a chirruping sound and pushed against Duncan's hand, encouraging more scratches.

"He'll make you do that all day if you don't watch out," laughed Faith. "Come on. Get in the van. Time to go home." She patted the side of the mobile library.

"I'll get the portal book!" said Kit, excitedly browsing the shelves to find the computer book they'd used to get here.

"Kit, excited about books," said Josh, shaking his head. "It's a funny old world.

Back at their own library, they decided to check up on the "mess" Lizzie claimed to have left behind before they all went home. When they reached the park gate, the sight that met them was madness. The park was crawling with talking animals. Not just talking – some of them were singing. A flock of green parakeets was singing a rude version of the national anthem. Fish from the lake were riding on the backs of terrapins. A troop of ants had formed a marching band.

And, what was worse, ordinary people were

noticing it. Sunburned people were wandering around in a daze, pointing at animals and blinking.

"I think I have sunstroke," one woman was saying.

"Must have drunk too much at that picnic," another man was saying.

"We need to shut this down, NOW," hissed Faith. "A magic-calming spell for starters. Kit, repeat it after me, and go the other way round the park. Each time you cast it, it should affect every animal within earshot."

"*Ruo onwe gi*," said Faith.

When Faith finished, the parakeets stopped singing and went back to chirping. The fish plopped back into the lake. The ants on the ground stopped chattering.

Kit listened carefully, then copied Faith, repeating the spell and doing the gestures – with Alita and Josh in tow, correcting her pronunciation when she got it wrong.

As they passed, and Kit cast her spell, the animals went back to normal. Any people they passed looked dazed, shaking their heads.

When they'd gone all round one half of the park, they met up with Faith again, who'd finished her half and was sitting on a bench by the gate. "All done?" she said.

Kit nodded. "What about the people? Were you putting a forgetting spell on them?"

"No need," said Faith. "In hot weather like this, people will convince themselves it was all in their heads. If this had been winter, when people are sharper, we would've been in trouble. So say thanks to the sunshine!" She gestured to the sky, turning up her face to the lowering sun.

Just then a dog trotted past, following a larger dog, and said, "I smell a nice bum!"

Kit blushed. "Er … I think I missed that one."

"It's OK. I've got it," said Faith. She said the spell one last time, and the dog stopped talking and started barking.

"So," said Kit. "We defeated the ghost rats from the dawn of time. We saved the mermaids from a curse, sent Lizzie home and helped Dogon too. What do we do next? How do we get ready in case they come back?"

"We do what we've *been* doing," said Faith. "We learn. We train."

"And we read?" said Josh.

"And we read," laughed Faith.

"Yay!" said Alita.

"Whatever else changes. Whatever threats we face," said Faith. "We will always have books."

Kit was surprised to find that she found that very comforting indeed.

ACKNOWLEDGEMENTS

The idea of a solitary genius writer is nonsense - every book is a team effort. This is my team.

Thanks to Polly, my agent, for all the support and encouragement. Thank you to Davide, my co-creator, who adds layers to my characters that I hadn't even imagined, from lumberjack shirts to 8-bit style scenes. Thank you to Tom, my editor, for preventing my characters from exploding like Mr Creosote due to an improbable number of meals, even though it pained him to take away cake from a story.

Thank you to Elisabetta, my designer, and to the whole Nosy Crow team who make, sell, promote, market and generally push my books into the world. Rebecca, special thanks to you for something that's not technically about this book – but for all your help getting book one out there. I'm sorry I didn't bring you back any gingerbread from Grasmere.

Thank you to my early readers, Ammara and Samantha, for shaping the world of the Library with me.

Thank you to the Girls, as always, and the Puppies, who know all the secrets and must keep our pact of mutually assured destruction. Thank you to Team Swag for all the cheerleading and for Cowell Finn. Thank you to Aisha and the rest of the gang, for an outlet. Thank you to the pocket friends, for higs. And thank you to the entire internet, especially those 30-50 feral hogs, for distracting me when writing was too hard, until I was ready to face it again.